MW00716315

A Bridge of Leaves

Prose Series 42

Diana Cavallo

A Bridge of Leaves

A Novel

Afterword by Mary Jo Bona

Guernica
Toronto/Buffalo/Lancaster
1997

Copyright © 1961, by Diana Cavallo and Atheneum.
Copyright © 1997, by Diana Cavallo
and Guernica Editions Inc.
Afterword © 1997, by Mary Jo Bona.
All rights reserved. No part of this book may be reproduced,
stored in a retrieval system, or transmitted, in any form or by
by any means, without the written permission of the
publisher.

Antonio D'Alfonso, Editor.
Guernica Editions Inc.
P.O. Box 117, Station P, Toronto (ON), Canada M5S 2S6
250 Sonwil Drive, Buffalo, N.Y. 14225-5516 U.S.A.
Gazelle, Falcon House, Queen Square, Lancaster LA1 1RN U.K.
Printed in Canada.

Legal Deposit — Fourth Quarter.
National Library of Canada
Library of Congress Catalog Card Number: 96-78719

Camadian Cataloguing in Publication Data
Cavallo, Diana
A bridge of leaves
(Prose series ; 42)
First published New York : Atheneum, 1961.
ISBN 1-55071-051-6
I. Title. II Series.
PS3553.A919B75 1997 813'.54 C97-900420-9

To Hiram Haydn

Beau ciel, vrai ciel, regarde-moi qui change!
Paul Valéry,
"Le Cimetière marin"

Part One

When I got up this morning and looked in the mirror, I was not in the least surprised to see my reflection, as I always do. It seemed a perfectly natural thing to be confronted by a picture of oneself that doesn't actually exist, or that exists only in relation to other things, perhaps they also assumed. But the whole thing must be got started in the first place, and just by acknowledging that image without controversy, we are already off—so why not?

After all, we believe quite thoroughly every external form. If I tell you I am within months of thirty, am average-sized, have dark hair, deep-set eyes—even embellish it a bit to say what *kind* of dark hair and *how* my eyes are set in my invisible but omnipresent skull—you are very likely, with only that much, to begin to draw a picture of me yourself. If I am skillful enough, I may even convince you of my reality, and we would get along quite well, you feeling satisfied that you already know something of me, and that being far from the case! It would be totally false; you would know nothing of me, and I want more than anything to impart my presence, beyond the form of it, although you hardly expected company the moment you sat down with a book, presumably to be alone. And yet, I will be content if you know relatively little of that external me, and satisfy yourself more with those parts that I would not readily show if I did not feel we were as alone as you thought when you settled down to hear me out.

I should warn you, so that you will not misunderstand when I wander off course, that I intend to talk about things quite as they strike me, but with a purpose all my own. You see, despite everything, I am trying to understand myself, a very ambitious undertaking, especially when I am so contradictory. I am sometimes tiresome, stuffy, and the next moment incredibly poetic or surprisingly humorous. It is very confusing to my friends, and so doubly so to me, who must maintain a semblance of order all the same.

I like to talk and I like to write, and I have such an enormous store of impressions and ideas that I feel weighted down with the load of it. Some of them are not meant to be passed on in conversation. Who nowadays talks about the manifoldness of life and death waiting? It would be considered embarrassing, self-conscious, more than a little naïve. Not that I am going to say such things, not outright, in any case, but I plan to go ahead and say what touches me at the moment or what I am reminded of, regardless of its order or disorder. I don't want to give a mistaken impression, because I want to represent myself and this undertaking in their true light. Yet I want very much to make the right beginning.

Do my intentions seem somewhat indefinite, even contradictory? I am different from what I seem, even here, so different that it is mysterious. The different selves I am are what is mysterious, the ones that I have been, that have been discarded somewhere, until I am so conventionally like other people that there seems hardly a difference between my individual form and theirs.

For I am overlaid with what I have become, and to restore any semblance of the past, I must try to enter it as best I can from this present state, incorporating as much of those other selves as still persist somewhere. It becomes all the harder because thoughts and moments sometimes become so separate from one another, and from what I now am, that I barely remember they belong to me. They vaguely resemble some other that was never me, the one that I imagine myself to be, that is fast disappearing even as I try to fold it into the page.

It is off again; perhaps it has lighted somewhere in these musings, remembrances, or more than likely, it will pass from page to page as my pen does, impressing a little of itself on the rough sheets; but that tiny insect, it will fly the cover. It is nowhere tied fast, secure, not even in these poor pages where I hear his faint buzzing and follow the meandering sound into the night.

(1)

THE amazing thing is that man wants to live, that he does not actively wish to die, that he would rather breathe in foul air, propagate imbecile children, spread contagion to his neighbor, and not rebel against such unnatural acts. As for me, I am surprised that, all things considered, I do not find it more pointless than I do.

Certainly, I have expended much less energy and interest in the matter than its importance warrants. But perhaps I think I will have an excess of such feeling when I am old, and should experience it for myself. But then, the old people that I know seem so reluctant to die. There is my grandfather, for example, an incredible old man of eighty-six who is mortally afraid of death. He suffers the most intense pain in his arms and legs, but prefers it to any thought of his eventual demise. He complains that he is the only one left of his generation; each year has taken one or the other of his friends; he feels out of place and alone in a strange world of youth and activity. Does this move him to a monumental death wish? No, he clings to life as though it were a precious thing, too valuable to resign. Fear makes it so, but still, I doubt that I shall have such spirit or such capacity to be afraid when I am old. I even feel a little cheated. It seems young people like myself have less of everything—less contentment, less pain, less serious ambition, less pride of achievement. We have too much of some things, but too little of these others. We do nothing to acquire the worth while ones; we only resent not having them. I wonder—if my grandfather had not worked at his trade for fifty years, would he have had them, anyway?

When I stop to consider what my grandfather has to live for, I am at a loss for reasons. What precisely goes on in his mind I can never know. Certainly I cannot ask him. In the first place, he looks at me, already intractable when I address him, surmising that I am an unintroduced stranger or a tax collector. He has become very sensitive about money, and has felt since he was eighty that his Olympian age entitled him to be tax-free. In any case, it is not until I am with him for an hour or so that he realizes I am one of the family. Then he insists I am Lily's older boy, and when I insist that I am David, Helen's son, he sputters that Helen never married. To convince him otherwise is hopeless.

He has lost all his teeth and refuses to replace them. He eats soft foods and becomes so irritated with their taste and texture that he splatters them about the table like a child. He insists conversation helps to pass the time, but he dozes every few minutes, napping fitfully through the day, so there is no continuity to his hours. But at night, when he is alone and weary, he is afraid to close his eyes and sits heavy-lidded in a faded armchair, stamping his foot or waving his arm to deter death and convince himself he is still alive.

In his wakeful afternon hours he can never find what he is looking for. He accuses his daughter-in-law of hiding his things, and has driven her voice up to a shrill pitch, so that her presence is intolerable to him. In between all these exasperations, he has a traveling pain that attacks a different limb or vital organ each day. It is not localized, so he can never complain of his poor stomach regularly, releasing his antagonism on a single malady. He frequently writhes or moans as the pain traverses his frail body, so that it has become intolerable to all of us, each one hoping he will depart quietly in his sleep that night. This is precisely why he will not go to bed or close his eyes at evening. He fears death in the darkness of his vigil, as though it never comes at noon. He is like some parents who take all precautions to safeguard their daughters in the evening, as though illicit love were banished by the daylight.

I almost prefer the intense striving after death of the early Christian martyrs, the blessed release, the marriage with God, the return to the eternal womb, and all of that. Of course, with such religious zeal for death, it would be hard to rule out suicide as the Desert Fathers did.

It seems that one is always confronted with that choice—one either wishes it fiercely or fears it intensely! Surely, there must be a middle course, some ground that someone as modern and conventional as I might tread—somewhere between a prayerful St. Anthony and a senile grandfather—without feeling one has avoided the issue entirely, stupidly pretended it does not exist. And yet, it is supposed that people who are not religious give the matter no thought, and that those who are young do not actually conceive it.

I know I speak only for myself, but I insist such reflections are bound to occur. Can one really pass to manhood without some jolt, some jar, that places it squarely before him? One must dislodge the nettle, whatever the means.

Perhaps, then, my first reaction was hasty and untrue. We are involved with it whether we wish it or not. Having put aside those questions which answer themselves, and those answers which frame the next question, one must prepare to ponder death with questions unformed, let alone answers, and that takes the greater effort. Perhaps here the largest number turn back to old paths once abandoned.

And I fear we are burdened too long with an incomprehensible morality, remonstrated too soon for acts unknown and thoughts unfelt, filled with vague fears for the world's transgressions, not yet knowing our connection with the world. Yes, I knew that exaltation as a child, of being dipped in the concrete of penance, sinking in the swamp briar of confession, disappearing beneath the sin-filled lake, arms outstretched in supplication. To be reclaimed at the bottom of the sea, to be disengaged from the morass of the flood plain, to reappear in the pure waters of the baptismal fount a cleansed soul, a purged heart, a resurrected body! But once frame the last question, and all the waters of the world flooding the cavity left bleeding by the moon cannot cleanse our limbs of doubts encrusted by purposeless life. Baptismal founts run dry, send rusted water, tepid and brown, to drown the unalterable stain fashioned by manhood. Confession consoled the unquestioning child; penance redeemed his sinless heart. They fail the man.

(2)

I HAVE had days when I was two persons at once, not merely the possibility of a second self, but the actuality. People are always trying to make out something else from what one says, and I have said quite simply what I mean.

Have I said I was a twin? I was the elder by several minutes. I lived; the other, delicate from birth, died at two years. I have since had days when I was both of us, and had conversations with my brother, grown tall as I am. I had never had the least recollection of him or the least realization that he had existed. He was, rather, a curious, rarely mentioned occurrence of long ago, until, when I was six, he became a reality, a still present force to remain forever with me.

We were visiting New England, and a German lady who had seen me as an infant came to call. I was in my room in a strange house, fascinated by my ignorance of the relatives with whom we stayed. I peeked into the living room and was made much of by the visitor, who kissed me twice and gave me peppermint to remember her. Becoming flustered, I went to my mother, who soothed my feelings, straightened my new clothes, and sent me out to play. Outside I discovered boys my age and they invited me to join their game. I ran inside to change my clothes, and came downstairs in old pants and sneakers, my hair tousled from the hurried yank of a sweat shirt over my head.

The German lady was leaving and paused at the stair well, blocking my exit.

"Here is the other one," she exclaimed. "Yes, yes, there were two, and so alike. This must be the healthier. His color is much better. Both lovely boys!" She beamed at my mother, whose eyes had fallen and whose arm fluttered and reached for the wall to support her. My aunt was beside her at once and spanned her shoulders with a firm grip.

"That's David—it's still David. The other one—has died." My aunt's voice was a strident burst of outrage, both at this absurd mistake and my complicity in its occurrence.

The lady's face grew stiff, a rigidity transformed her features, stopping her trembling mouth, pasting her bulging eyes, straightening her sagging back. Then, wordlessly, she turned and ran, leaving the screen door banging back and forth behind her.

How peculiar it was to be taken for two persons, to house at once two separate beings, for it to be possible at all. The place seemed strange, the people were out of a dream, and dreamlike, I was the spectator, the curious onlooker who contained the others, the space, the image, in himself, without being at one with them. And out of this submersion for an instant came consciousness of that other dead self, the lost blood stream, the complementary nervous system, the dissolved will, my brother.

Who has ever dreamed a dead thing awake has pressed the nerve cell of the natural world, has pried primordial memory loose from distant moorings, has found the umbilicus of hungering life and voiceless death. The brother I impersonated unknowingly, unsuspecting we postulate a personality or two or three or myriad forms or facets of a self, was lifelike a few seconds. Which was he, I asked—the scrubbed and bashful boy for whom the social world was pain, or the re-energized one who craved companionship and games? How many times has man surprised himself and been puzzled by a severance in the familiar whole, the known entity he was? For me, thenceforth, there was a retreat from this unanswered question. There was one who shared with me the undulating wall that antedated exposure to the world, who, in the rhythm of birth, alternated with me the giant seizures which brought me unwilling to the light, he following on my heels. Is there a rival experience that draws two people closer, to be more totally at one with another life? The act of love which joins two souls, two transfigured beings touching one another's synapses; the state of pregnancy in which one body gives of itself to form another, makes way for it, nourishes it—these are the acme of integration, supreme states of oneness in the world. Still, they are two, the lovers entwined, and the mother kindling the sperm into the emerging foetus. But we were one—one thought, one act, one seed, a single cell sundered by the overheat of generation, and by the pressure of the finite will pulsating in the bloodstream.

In moments of estrangement from the mask of David, there rises in me the stamen silk of Michael, born to the world, reclaimed, made unborn again by it, but still borne in me in that one, vast rebirth, the world of human memory.

(3)

As far back as I can remember my grandmother said of my grandfather: "He was a dandy in his day. He could spend hours fussing with the style of his mustache or the knot of his tie." Now we could barely force him to change his food-stained clothes, and the barber, a close friend of the family, would hold him fast in his chair when he shaved him twice a week. My grandmother, who had grown fleshy and wrinkled with age, took little care of her appearance when I knew her. She wore faded house-dresses sizes too large for her, and hairpins jutted out of the mound of streaked hair piled on her head. Yet there were photographs of her as a young girl and on her wedding day. Her hair, thick and black, hung to her shoulders, and her hips were slim under the white satin folds.

How curious that they were the same, the vain philanderer and the flatulent old man, the intense young innocent and the wise, worn matron. They bore the vaguest resemblance to one another, as though distantly related, the man great-uncle to the boy, the woman grand-cousin to the girl. That this is what they had become in fifty years seemed a perverse stroke, so that, comparing them, I could understand the despair and rage of ancient Greek citizens who deduced they were the puppet victims of idle gods.

As a young girl my grandmother dreamed of a simple life of relative ease with a large affectionate family and a prosperous husband. But dreams can lie; pitilessly they remain with us when they have been stripped of truth to taunt us with our own desire and the supple shape and warm flesh we have given them. So, exiling her dreams to this half-life of reverie, she married a handsome man of inconstant attentions and little means and fled with him to the New World, where they were poorer still and strangers besides. She told me how she wept, stammering the brittle sounds of a new tongue that flushed waves of Mediterranean homesickness through her with each rough syllable.

Now that I think of it, my grandmother's was the first inner world I discovered. I felt her pulse before I knew my own; lying against her chest I could hear the rhythm of her life in the crease of her neck, and I took it for my own which was silent in the child's world of becoming. I read thoughts in her face before I was capable of forming them myself, and while all my emotions were undifferentiated, blandly the same; in her, I felt all the variety and subtlety of a populated world. Her displeasure had infinite forms and faces—a grimace, a wince, a cold stare, a heavy voice, a passionless grunt, an implacable stillness. Her gaiety brought her close to my own few years, and she would pick a wisp of hair from her face as though she were an absorbed child interrupting a flood of activity with this hasty gesture of self-consciousness. The hand arrested in that familiar movement, or doubled over in the concentrated kneading of yellow dough for the pastry delicacies we loved, or faintly stirring while she talked in the unalterable rhythm of crochet work—one hand supersedes the other, and now there is a montage of hands, to stand for her, strong and lined, tanned from out-of-doors and veined from heavy work, ever-moving, ever-quick, metamorphosed into echoless bits of petrified wood in the repose of sleep and in the consummation of the bier.

I have wondered many times how life could cease for her in whom I heard it swell and felt it quicken. I would have protested once that I would perceive and sense even a minute alteration in her being, so attuned were we to one another. But who is attuned to death? The eye that uncovers anger is blind, the ear that detects irritation is deaf, the mechanism that absorbs the minutiae of change is inert to the massive invasion of death. Perhaps there is ground for belief, as some authors say, that we carry death within us, and it waits the years for its time. Or, if not that, it takes up residence shortly before it retires with its load, to become accustomed to its place of assignment, and to prepare and lay siege to its host.

I had grown used to subtlety, so that I did not discern the sweeping changes that transformed her within weeks. We visited of mornings, the same as always, and walking beside her, I played the game of scrutiny—she held her head to the side, just so; this would be a day of funny stories, of riddles and puns with me, of many brushes of her fingers at my side. Or if she blinked her eyes and walked erect, I knew her to be out of sorts, and I waited for her to wrench my hand as we ran across the street, and to purse her lips as we approached the door, just so, in a slightly peevish gesture. With such a game as that, how could I stop to notice the wanness of her face, the sinking of her eyes, the gauntness of her cheeks, the heaviness of her step, the shortness of her breath? So we strolled together, I unsuspecting. And she? I would have known if she knew.

(4)

I SUPPOSE that ever since I was a child I had heard of people dying one way or another. It was even said by old ladies who drank demitasses with my grandmother that it was a pity that I was the only child that had lived. This was before I had re-fashioned Michael into the lively voice of our dia-logues, in the days when words were disconnected sounds that blew out of our mouths. These words had stirred only a passing curiosity that I soon for-got because I had always been considered the only child, and I could not imagine that it had not always been so. On this occasion my grandmother made a motion with her hand to silence her friends and gave a quick look at me to see if I had heard. I sucked in my milk-soaked bread and twined my feet around the stout chair legs. The conversation drifted to the illness of an old woman of ninety-three who had outlived both her sons. My grandmother said it was a terrible thing for a parent to remain and the off-spring to be taken. A fly was buzzing around the cinnamon cake and I caught at it, thinking how strange the talk of my elders seemed, how long they could sit and discuss topic after topic, how slowly the words came from the cracked brown lips of my grandmother's friends.

One day we were in the grocery store, and as I left the candy counter I heard the grocer say that she had lived a full life after all and no one could expect to live forever. My grandmother said it was nice to go in one's sleep like that; all deaths should be so painless. Someone came up and said the relatives couldn't decide who should pay for the funeral. Wasn't that awful, said the grocer, not to have common decency? The woman said that people had grown crass and it was a shame to be living in such troubled times. My grandmother said it was sad and perhaps the neighbors could get up some money. But the grocer protested the family should take care of that, and besides business was bad again.

Once my father took us driving in the park. It was a treat for me because he seldom had time away from his work. Several times he looked through the rear-view mirror and told me to keep my head in and sit down. It seemed as though we were going faster when I leaned my head out and the wind rushed in my ears. We had just turned the corner when we saw a large crowd gathered in the street. People pressed against one another and stood on tiptoe to see beyond the rows of craned necks in front of them. My father stopped the car and tried to pry a few words from the bystanders, who answered in monosyllables and did not even turn their heads as they spoke. I could hear a low moan, and then men with stretchers were pushing through the crowd with practiced efficiency. After they had disappeared into the place that had opened for them and closed again around them, we heard a shriek, a woman's violent screams filled the park. A man at the back of the crowd turned away and walked toward the car where we peered out the window. "They were out walking, and he fell. He just dropped dead. He was younger than I am." He shook his head as the woman's screams subsided into sobs. "It could happen to anyone," my father said, and we drove away.

Though I pressed my head against the window-pane and stroked my lips in concentration the day my grandmother died, I could think of no other times when I had heard the name of death or espied his faint figure behind a conversation.

No one wanted to tell me my grandmother had died. It is a difficult task for an adult who has never spoken to a child of death, and who, at middle age, having lost a friend or two and members of the family, has had his first encounter with the final questions. Though still unspeakable, one is called upon to speak. There is the child. Something grave has happened. Several people have looked in at the door to see if he is still asleep. There is much going in and out, and each time the door closes as though muted, carefully held as it makes its accustomed arc, and is shut. All is busyness and quiet at the same time. People are talking, but in a hoarse whisper. A neighbor stands by the kitchen stove, dropping carrots and celery into the soup. They all turn and stare at the boy who has come into the room. Someone leaves the room; someone begins to cry; someone lowers his head; someone says, "Come here, David, and have your breakfast."

What has happened that has made it so solemn? Eyes are red from crying; some tears are still coming and are pushed away by the back of the hand. Now they are talking. They have decided to send me to Aunt Lily's. I will have my breakfast there. I can see my cousins and we can dress up and play in the attic. But what is wrong? No one will answer, and they run to find my coat and hat and get the car ready. It must be something terrible. Perhaps they found I have a horrible disease that can't be cured and is contagious and they are sending me away, maybe forever. Or, perhaps, they discovered something I did, something shameful, and they can't bear to look at me. Perhaps someone saw me in the cloak-room at school when I was by myself, and my mother told me never to do that. Suddenly I want to cry, and I have begun to sniffle. I want someone to comfort me, to love me even if I have ruined the world and am black with sin. "Where is Grandmom?" I cry out. There is a hush; even the tears are stilled; their eyes are on me. Which one will answer? Why is it so dreadful? Where is my grandmother?

My Aunt Lily takes my hand; she whispers to my father she must tell me; she stoops over to look in my face. "Your grandmother has gone away, far away, where we can't see her any more. But we mustn't feel sad, because she's happier there. It's a wonderful place where everyone wants to go some-day." I nod my head. Aunt Lily turns away. Then why are they crying? Why is your voice cracking, Aunt Lily? It must be that she is dead. But what is dead? The old lady across the street was ninety-three and she was sick a long time. The man died in the park, but he had an ambulance and a stretcher. Can I see my grandmother if I want to? Maybe they are wrong. Maybe if I wait, she will come. Maybe she has gone away like she did last year to see Uncle Peter. But she'll be back. But they said we won't see her any more. She is dead— Perhaps I ought to go to Aunt Lily's, and they will tell me what it is. Perhaps they all want me to go so they will stop crying and someone will talk to me soon.

In those days people had the viewing at home. The dead were laid among familiar things, so that death itself was the only strangeness, and if one wept or screamed or fainted, it was a family affair and not a public gesture. I have been to many viewings since: in vaultlike rooms where people file in and out, in ornate palatial chambers where friends commiserate in plush, upholstered chairs, in replicas of churches where mourners kneel formally in pews. But the kindest and the cruelest, the most vivid and the most remote is still the one in the home where I grew up, when all who knew her came to pay respects to my grandmother.

They would not have let me go, but I asked to see her in a quiet voice, and there was no one to refuse so simple and so imperative a request. I wore a dark-blue suit and new shoes with an echo of a squeak in them. I rode in my uncle's car, and approached the house from the outside as any visitor might do. But once inside, it was my home, with everything I knew where I remembered it. The peo-

ple sitting and standing in the hall and in the rooms I
hardly noticed, though I knew each one well and
saw them for the first time all together, like this,
in so unusual a combination. What struck me most
on entering the living room was that it should be
there at all and looking quite as it always did. I had
thought, the last few days, wondering alone what
would become of me, that everything was altered
forever, that the outside of things could never look
the same because the inside had changed so completely. My parents kissed me, and I felt for them
a new love that one shares for hurt things. I noticed
no other faces really, only eyes that met mine or
pressed on me from the outside, or looked past me to
the heavy, black box on the floor. It was then I saw
it clearly, its solidness and its woodenness, and I was
relieved that it would hold, and could be trusted to
perform its rite. I stared at it with the fascination
and respect I had known for the sturdy wooden
bucket that descended the deep, dark well on a farm
I visited. It struck me that these two things were very
much the same, because my cousin had told me they
would send a box down deep into the earth, very far
down where it was dark, and that was where my
grandmother would be. And standing by the open
bier, I said to myself, Here is the box, here is my
grandmother, and here am I.

There was a wisdom in old embalmers who never
strove to put the flush of life in pallid cheeks. There
was the look of death in her; I could not mistake
it for sleep or believe that it was temporary. I knew
in that one moment what I had not understood
when she had died and what I have never known so

positively since that day: that she was truly and forever dead.

(5)

MY DEAD now were two. One barely known but
felt deeply once on the stair well of a strange house,
the other known best of all things in the world and
most loved. I sought them both in the way men
seek the lost and hidden and remain nursing the
hollow search. For reminiscence is an old mistake,
old as the loneliness of men, and aching with the
dead weight of empty forms and shadow shapes.

Of all things, I craved Michael in the long year
following my grandmother's death. With him there
were none but new ties, which could be forged
along the way. I yearned to find him and feel him
alive again in me as I had encountered and absorbed
him not quite four years before. But though I might
think of him, concentrating fiercely on his name, or
asking ravenous questions about him, so that, im-
bibing things known of him, I might invoke his
presence, still I did not experience that Michael who
I knew was possible, whom I had known with such
fullness and awareness at the stair rail.

A peculiar thought has occurred to me of those
childhood days. What I had found on the stair well
was a discovery, something which for me had never
before existed. Yet Michael had existed once, and

though I had no memory of him, there were others who did, and who perhaps thought of him still. No doubt they pictured him with the full, soft face of the two-year-old he had been, his limbs still trembling with the excitement of each step, his lips still seeking the shape of words to find the sound. But I saw him full-grown as I was, identical to me as we once were, only a little thinner because he had been more delicate. So it would seem that those who knew him in life cherished a truncated image, while I, who knew him only in death, participated in a miraculous resurrection, where he grew and changed as I experienced.

Another full realization of Michael did not come until I was almost ten. And then it was unexpected; it was when I was no longer trying actively to rediscover him that he suddenly appeared.

I remember that one Sunday I was sent to church alone. It had been my wont to go each Sunday with my mother, but this Sunday no one accompanied me. As I walked alone, I felt again the quickening excitement of another day when I had walked this same route in the boys' procession for my First Communion. My dark-blue suit had been new then, and the flower in my lapel had tiny drops of water shining on the blossom. It was the same suit that I had worn the next year, with the cuffs let out for my grandmother's viewing. The suit was worn out now, and I had come home one day from school startled to see it at the top of the trash heap, sooty and wrinkled, to be burned at the city dump. Here I was, proceeding toward the church in other clothes, feeling only slight traces of those discarded ones, knowing perhaps that the crease fell in the same place, and that was all.

The church was just ahead. I knew because the street and pavement were crowded with people over there, and the steps were covered with little bunches of figures that diminished in size toward the top until they were only tiny dots and specks at the door. There were bright flounces of color that alternated with somber hues and lighter tones, so that it seemed from afar a mammoth pattern design that ran from the top of the steps to the crowded foreground of color spilling into the street. I walked past and saw everything close and in its true size and shape, so that, when I reached the corner and looked back, I wondered even more at the stunning effect it had from a distance, as of a huge and well-worked tapestry.

I was amazed that I had left the church behind. Though it had been the place where I was going, I had never stopped when I reached it, but continued walking, long past it, with no thought to where I would end. I crossed streets with unfamiliar names, and peered into darkened shops and odorless restaurants, walking where few people left the Sunday quiet of their homes and on down widening lanes that led to intersected streets heavy with buses and the thickening flow of traffic. Along the main artery I walked, my eyes everywhere at once, jumping across spaces to where knots of people had collected, like the groups and bunches I had left behind.

There they were, across the avenue, there where a block-long lot, once empty perhaps, was covered with large canvas tents and vending stands. People were already streaming onto a dirt path, and beyond them there were crowds lining up at ticket windows. Drawing near, I was swept into the moving throng of backs that walked toward something. In the jumble of voices I could hear the wobbling sound of music, swelling and dying, but quickened, speeded up . . . the animated breathing of a huge organ . . . the loud voices and strident laughter . . . the noise of the place . . . pressing against the people in front of me . . . moving toward an unknown prize . . . a haze of music drowning my thoughts. . . .

Tall men with rasping voices held out merchandise and made furry toys walk. Men with hot-dog wagons and ice-cream carts held their wares aloft. The longer I followed the crowd, the louder were all the sounds around me—the shouting, the echo of the frightened laughter and shrieks, hawking in my ear —they seemed to come not only from all sides of me, but from over my head. I followed the sounds that led me, that summoned me from above and pulled me to where they began.

I cut off from the crowd at a small enclosure where people leaned side by side over a railing, watching with fascination what was on the other side. I could not see what they were watching, and I stood behind the bent figures, waiting for the one in front of me to turn around and leave. I expected him to incline his head for a moment, to cross himself and rise wordlessly, never looking as he passed.

My hand on the rail, I watched in wonder as small glossy cars swished past, sweeping the laughing children and nervous girls from side to side, whirling them around corners with such speed that the tracks glistened and threw out tiny sparks. It was like an endless chase, around and around, springing and lurching, again and again, but none of the cars could overreach its leader, and when the match was over, they slowed to a finish, and stopped.

The collection envelope afforded me a wrinkled dollar bill, a pitiful specimen. I made my offering at the ticket window. I chose a bright-blue car and strapped myself in. Music began to belch from a perforated face above me and the car swirled into motion. Now the staring faces of which I had been one a moment ago were over there, watching the new I that was flung from side to side. There was the gleam of railing, but behind were rows and rows of pink carnations, their ridged faces peeping from a round floral display. And far to the left, where neon lights had blinked their sleepy scrawl, I spied the flickering play of tiny votive lamps, recording, with the rising and falling light, each dedicated prayer enshrined in ruby glass. Beyond them I could see dark picture booths with black curtains strung across the top, there where I had watched solitary figures go in and out to unburden their old faces to an unseen camera and emerge with bright new pictures of themselves. Jerked by the neck and thrown forward as the car whisked around the bends of track, whirled and buffeted, I felt hurled into that space of park on relentless wheels that churned ever faster, blurring the world about me, and sending a dizzying haze before my eyes. For all the lights were on and candles lit; white gleamed from the altar, and the gold of the chalice shone in the priest's hands. He

had made the sign of the Cross with giant strokes
and held a dim white wafer in his fingers. He moved
across the line of faces at the rail, offering and intoning, to stand at last before a young boy in a
dark-blue suit, a shining blossom in his lapel, waiting
with face upturned, eyes closed tight, and arms
crossed ready on his chest. Yes, he saw me as I
saw him. . . . With a smile and a faint flick of the
tongue, he held the airy, bodiless form in his mouth,
felt it grow heavy, congealing into a new shape, until with a swallow it dissolved into a sweetish presence that remained when all else had disappeared.

I dropped the cotton candy from my hand. It was
destroyed somewhere below as the car whirled round
and banished every form from sight. Again I knew
the sweep of motion and the exhilaration of the
chase. In the midst of blur I saw faces emerge behind
the rail, and the neon lights returned with their dim
red flicker, and the black curtains of the picture
booths opened and shut beyond. The car had slackened its pace; it too was breathless; with feeble
grunts and pants it strained forward and fell back
again, a final spurt and collapse.

I clutched the rail and stood staring around me
at the carnival and at myself among the pushing
throngs and glitter. I was surely there, and the church
was nowhere to be seen. I knew it to be blocks
distant where the Mass must be in Final Prayers
now. And the young boy who took Communion
with the white and gold shining on him must be
kneeling now, with the names of Michael, John, and
all the saints falling from his lips and joining the
gathering crescendo of voices to the final Amen. I

crossed myself as I thought he must be doing, aware that he was something apart from me, although I had looked at him as one looks upon oneself in a confused dream, with a shiver of recognition and an uncertain delight. Having known Michael through the whole sinews of my being that long-ago clutching at the rail, I would know him again if I saw him. There was no doubt that it was he, the boy leaning his chest reverently against the cold rail of the altar . . . Michael . . . already separated from me across a long distance, but known as I knew moments of myself.

Where had he fled those years when I sought him and he clung wraithlike to the hidden cogs of memory? How had we become separate, Michael and I, who were one once on the stair well and one once in the throbbing womb, dark as lost memory? He had seen me as I saw him over the neon lights into the sanctum of the altar. There, seeping into the exhilaration, the delight, the gratitude of rediscovery, was the quiet despair of loss, of slowly pulling away and being pulled from the whole being I was. The same exhilaration and despair—it must have been—that the seedling felt, pulled apart to form a new life in the chaos of growing too full for one shape. Here then was the excitement of rescuing twice-lost Michael from an obliterated world, together with the sorrowing knowledge that he might come again and again, but grow fainter, farther removed, and finally, one day, altogether separate from me.

It was, perhaps, this sad, full moment, the painful foreknowledge of the ferment in us, not yet ready, not yet complete, but coming . . . the white and red grapes ripening and the juices readying for the harvest.

(6)

I AM glad that it is in a moment of relative calm that I try to resurrect the Terror. Otherwise I might be so overcome that I could never describe or explain it. Even so, I find it harder to tell than any other thing, because, as I remember, it begins to fasten itself on me, and I can barely make the effort to move or to utter words to banish it.

But I must recall that it is a thing of the past, and summon up my breath without delay, staving off as I do the familiar, fearful drowsiness that besets me as I remember, so that I might tell you as well as I can of that terrible time.

For it was sometime after we had returned to our old house that I first came to know it. Only then did I realize that my life had become divided into two camps—my world by night and my world by day. There was no easy transition of one into the other, no moment when one might perceive with a casual glance that it had grown dark and could go about one's business without a further thought. I could no longer call my own that life of effortless continuity from one hour to the next and from day to day that is the blessed lot of most people, and that was mine once, too, before it was thrown out of balance by the Time of the Terror.

How can I describe the days? If I might lead you to a classroom window, I would search out a hunched shape, unremarkable among like hunched shapes, face resting on upturned palms, fingers flicking over unread pages, but with eyes suddenly alight and deeply smiling, and I could tell how his agile mind was fleeing down dark roadways and leaping over high places, and you would know that it was my image leaning on the desk, and my days that were described in those hot and flickering eyes.

But it was precisely the days that I could bear, and the nights that were unbearable. For it was the night that I strove to put off . . . to push farther away . . . to postpone altogether, the night and the moment when I would be forced to look at the face of the Terror.

This was exactly why I would remain downstairs reading long after all had retired, until my heavy eyes looked on a gelatinous page, or as an alternative, I might stay up writing letters to relations who had yet to answer my other nocturnal summons. Or I would occupy the bathroom interminably, so that the rest of the family would begin to call my name—all of this to postpone the agony of going to my room. Finally, there could be no further delay, and I entered with a pounding heart and downcast eyes, performing the necessities-before-retiring with a rit-ualistic sense of order and sequence. Now everything was finished. I had only to slide down between the sheets and reach up to snap off the lamp. This was the moment! Even if I had promised myself not to look up and to pretend it did not exist, assuming this semiprone position reminded me of nothing

else, so that the Terror would grip me—just a pang
at first, like a sudden momentary jab of pain in the
night, but within seconds I could feel nothing but
the stiffness of my whole body, stiff from the Terror.
And it would rise from my frozen toes and deaden
all in its wake, lifting my overcome eyelids to confront the shape on the ceiling.

Of course it was there . . . a brown, growing
thing . . . that thrust its feet out of the corner . . .
that had spindly legs and willowy arms . . . and
some kind of strange garment wrapped around it.
But I had to look closer . . . to be sure . . . for I
knew what might happen . . . and peering up at
it, I saw that there where the belly had been a beard
was forming, and above it the vague outline of a
face . . . but that other, the head in the corner
from which the first uncertain line had trickled . . .
it was only the clenched shape of a fist . . . the wob-
bly legs had closed to form a puffy sleeve . . . so
that I could no longer look at the shape from the
corner out . . . but from another direction altogether . . . because the other, thin unsteady creature visible for days, with perhaps a new flourish to
his costume, was barely visible . . . only my memory
and imagination could even suggest him there . . .
where this large puffy creature was emerging,
bearded and threatening, to press a heavy torso down
upon the first white seam of the paper. . . .

The Terror remained . . . for it was really this
. . . how it would never stay the same . . . and
when I thought I had come to know it, it would
change . . . I had to watch and watch each night
. . . growing used to the new one . . . and the rain

would come again. . . . With the procession of
nights it would become a different thing . . . I
could no longer see the thing I had got used to. . . .
I might say to myself, "It is only a brown stain,
rain dripping on a worn part of the roof." . . . But it
was the last thing I would see when I went to bed.
. . . It had invaded only my ceiling. . . . And when
I unfroze enough to snap on the light, thin slits of
light fell on the ceiling . . . a ladder or a trellis or
the long arms of railroad ties. . . . But it was no
use thinking of them or building other thoughts for
diversion . . . for soon the shaft of light would touch
the brown stain . . . and fire a moment the spindly,
wiry legs . . . but no, not now . . . now it would
light the tufts of beard or the large puffy sleeves . . .
I might look tomorrow . . . and it would be *that*
creature I would follow, and *he* would be the Terror . . . and for days after, I would watch him grow
and spread farther across the ceiling . . . until even
with the Terror, I came to know him and respect
him. . . . But one day the familiar shape would be
used to form the new one . . . and I would begin to
see it cover over and make use of the other . . . for
that was the Terror . . . the watching and the
change . . . the brown stain advancing and always
there . . . the last thing at night . . . never the
same . . . forever watching . . . feeling it watching . . . a strange one . . . a new shape . . . the
old one gone . . . and the new . . . and . . . always . . . and changing . . . and . . . sleep.

For it was sleep I wanted—that was the comfort
and the refuge. But I would have done anything to
put off the Terror, to drag out the tired day, so that

night would never come, and with it the Terror.

I have thought of my grandfather just now. It seems right that I do so when I recall this time of my life, for it seems that those who have found it too hard to grow old and strain against the magnetic pull of death have much in common with rebellious youths who strain against the manhood forced on them that impels them into a feared and unknown world. Then, too, it has occurred to me that I should look with new eyes on my grandfather's fears of the night, and that I should remember to let him doze on fitfully by the window when all have retired for the night. I can conspire with him to prolong the day as I used to do, and hold back as long as possible the dark night.

(7)

THAT old man sat dozing today, almost tranquilly, except for little snorts erupting from him—even breath was an act of feeble combat.

I could not help staring at him in the most unabashed way, for I had seen his faded blue face so long without looking at it that I had never missed the moisture that is in other faces. Yet, the fluid gone, his body and his bones past help of daily lubrication, his skin was not stiff and dry as one might expect, but from weakness and tiredness it had fallen and gathered limply around the pockets of the skull.

I had not looked at him with such intense scrutiny

and immense bewilderment for thirteen years, when, I think, I saw him for the first time—very briefly but memorably—for I have carried that isolated evening with me a long time.

Then, too, I had sat across from him and had let my eyes and thoughts wander over him as though he were a dumb thing, an unreflecting object. Thirteen years ago, at seventy-three, he seemed so ancient, already bent over, his teeth gone. I, at sixteen, coming into the house and seeing him from afar, used the words "doddering" and "decrepit" in my mind as he walked to the sofa with a shuffle, his legs apart. At school we had been learning of the evolution of man, and seeing him, I thought to myself that as we grow old we resemble those unsteady quadrupeds who, with enormous effort, had pulled themselves upright, but who, on the slightest pretext, slumped back in comfort toward the solid earth.

My grandfather had rejoined his sister on the couch. I had come in too late for the embraces and the sighs, the tears and high-pitched screams which, I was sure, had accompanied their first meeting in forty-two years. The entire family had gathered at the house for the occasion early in the morning, for the rattle of pots and smell of garlic had not ceased since I awoke, and I gathered up myself and my books for an afternoon of study at the library. I had been irritated all day by this mass intrusion into the house and by the thought that here was the long-awaited Midsummer Night that had beguiled me ever since I'd read the famous play at school. Now I would be spending so magical a night with old uncles and aunts and cousins younger than I was.

I came back on purpose after the grand arrival of my grandaunt. I had heard her described as the youngest of the family, a slim, lovely woman much like my mother—my grandfather's favorite in a houseful of brothers and sisters. Now that my gaze fell on her, I was startled to see a woman as old as my grandfather, perhaps even more lined and wrinkled than he from the warm but scarring sun, with braids of thick, all-white hair set in a mound on her head. She and my grandfather were oblivious of my presence across from them, so I remained sitting there, listening to the complex rhythm of their speech, their hands, and their mobile, restless faces. They chattered in a rich Italian dialect, my grandfather speaking in the same mellifluous accent as his sister, leaving all the endings on the words as though they belonged there, his voice rising and falling with a phrase, like an incantation. I had heard his Italian before, the truncated, garbled sound of the old men on street corners, a far different sound from this one emanating without effort from him.

The two of them laughed most of the time, and my grandfather leaned his head to the side and tapped his knee all the while, in what must have been an old characteristic gesture, for his sister remarked on it, and they laughed again. But it was something I had never seen him do; familiar and a part of him as it was, it had nothing to do with me or with the grandfather I had lived with for years.

For the first time since my grandmother died, I was glad I could understand the language I thought I had buried with her. My grandfather was singing

a song they used to sing as children, proud of remembering every word, and still off key, his sister
said. They recounted stories of their village, of their
farm, and of each other, one beginning and flaming
the other's memory, so that they often spoke at the
same time, with no apparent contradiction, but in
chorus—one rocking back and forth, one sharing
the other's reminiscence with a soft, happy groan of
"yes, oh yes—ah, so it was—yes, yes."

As they spoke I could make out the out-of-doors
they lived in—the hot sun, and the stony, cragged
land that had to be worked by hand, the small
cramped farm overrun with shouting groups of
children who worked their high spirits into the
soil they turned as they talked and laughed together.
Or again, I could see the village square nearby where
old men sat and smoked together, and the younger
ones doused one another's heads in the fountain to
overcome the heat, and on the path to the village
square were large families of children ranging the
roads in search of nuts or berries or buckets of much-
needed manure. My grandfather could not stop
laughing as he remembered the favorite family pun-
ishment of long and solitary exile over the steaming
manure heap.

They were full of this life, those two crowded
together on the couch. I sensed it was no mere cast-
away existence or outgrown childhood, but real and
close enough to be touched with the hand, as they
often touched theirs when they wept quietly over the
loss of this or that loved one.

I felt, without moving, something of me going
toward them, to encounter not the wrinkled, bent old

man, nor the white-haired, age-lined sister, but the straight and robust young people they still saw themselves to be, who stared back at me midway between the ancient forms and my entranced, startled self.

I had no doubt that when those two old people saw one another for the first time in forty-two years, they had not even seen each other's faces, nor the lines and veins of age, but had fallen on a familiar sturdy frame and kissed familiar eyes that to them were unblemished and unscarred and as new as the days they had seen. Even I, as I watched, made out a coy girl who rolled her eyes and sighed, and a hearty, strapping youth who moved his arms agilely in telling a story, so that I knew they had once cleared fields, chopped wood, and cracked stones.

I shut my eyes, thankful that I was there for the Midsummer Night change to have been worked for me. In those withered limbs before me were a life and form that flowed freely once, freer than the drying fluid in a now cracking frame—a life and form that must still be there somewhere, even today, behind a faded blue face and sententious snorts in an armchair.

Today, as I looked at him sleeping fitfully, all his eighty-six years a heavy weight upon him, a line for each year on his creased face, I longed for a second momentary, mad glimpse of that other young world that only the high Midsummer moon could give.

(8)

R I T E S of initiation have always taken their own
particular form, though the ritual has always followed the ancient pattern of Adam and Eve. The
rites may have been more colorful in another era,
associated as they were with magic, religion, and
mysticism. Still, my initiation into the mysteries of
the physical were, perhaps, more in keeping with the
ancient spirit than most modern experiences of the
kind.

First, one must set the stage with Violet and Ann,
who belong to the secret world of one of my childhood years. The two, sisters—Violet my own age,
Ann slightly younger, our neighbors the year we
lived away from our old house—used to sit on the
adjoining porch, spreading their lessons earnestly
before them, both fair and blond, hair worn short
and straight, the kind of girls for whom a boy might
have a secret admiration that he won't admit to at
that early age. My mother thought them very sweet,
respectful the neighbors said, raising them higher
in esteem with each new courtesy and smile. As for
us, we got on well enough, but not so well as we
were meant to.

One rainy day when I had known them some
few months, I was mysteriously beckoned into their
basement den. The room was darkened; only candles spread their eerie shadows on the wall. The

girls were nowhere to be seen until they emerged
from behind a screen—a secret room, they fancied.
Both were dressed in costume, a sorceress' hat and
robe, and spread out cards to tell my fortune. They
spoke in whispers of high adventure in store for me,
a future of surprise and new discovery. Then, showing how far they had taken me into their confidence,
they led me by the hand into that secret room,
heavily draped, where they kept costumes and col-
lections. They set me before their treasure chest,
where, with mysterious smiles, they drew out a tiny
jewel box inlaid with two ivory pieces, which they
took up, still secretive, rubbing them tenderly and
dangling them before my eyes. At last, one of them
cradled them in her hand, shaking them there before casting them upon the table with a practiced
hand. There each piece came to rest after their sudden thrust forward, both heavily engraved with black
dots upon the ivory surface.

We gathered around the dice, as though they were
a magic force the girl's sorcery had created. And
then, with mounting excitement, we embarked upon
our game of chance, each watching tensely as the
others rolled, throwing them, at last, from our own
hand.

Violet won and turning cryptically to Ann, she
pointed. "I choose you." I wondered what was meant,
particularly when they exchanged a knowing smile.
Without another word, Ann flung open her robe
and produced the soft, white hump of a newly
emerging breast, which she thrust toward us proudly.
I looked from one tiny blond head to the other, while
they proceeded with the next round. Though I was

still speechless, my luck was unimpaired, and when I won, both girls confronted me eagerly.

"Well, which one?" they asked together in some suspense. Each heart-shaped face drew nearer to my side of the table.

"Violet," I blurted out.

Wriggling herself triumphantly, she brought out a firmer, fuller breast, which Ann and I gazed at wonderingly until she pushed it from sight.

In the third game, Violet won again, and they laughed in some excitement as she pronounced carefully, "Your turn." I became flushed, confused, quite weak from the force of their stares, and finally, trapped, I heaved open my shirt and showed a poor, brown nipple on a hairless chest. Violet trembled; Ann blanched.

"Stupid! Not that!"

They began to converge on me, shamelessly looking me down. I toyed with the idea of scrambling under the table and making an ignominious escape. But the idea was too debasing. On the other hand, my not-so-delicate blond friends seemed capable of every assistance to gain their end. With only a down-ward flick of a zipper, all could be saved. I bared myself to the world a little hesitantly. But there was no need for fear, for they were singularly impressed. I remember that, all atremble, they set another date for our venture into this hectic world of sensuality and chance.

These mysterious rites continued for several months. It grew to seem a secret life. For on the surface all seemed as before. The sisters leaned over books and sweetly smiled, so it seemed hardly they who grew so glittering in the eye and so daring in their games. And I who spoke to them in school or from the porch seemed barely different from before. But once inside their basement den, we assumed another air. They would find a costume for each time, and feverishly we would withdraw the dice, cast rounds, and proceed with these rites of initiation that to our minds must have been the heights or depths of orgy.

These came to an abrupt end when my family moved back soon afterward to our old house. The girls were inconsolable and so was I. We had been fast losing our innocence with each further satisfaction of curiosity. But like the original offenders in the Garden, we dreamed it was strangely worth the price.

(9)

THERE is a balcony on this old house that leans from the second story in the back and oversees the yard. A most unlikely sight nowadays, as out of fashion as the old three-story house we live in that was meant to house three generations at once, and remains only half used if it is not turned into apartments.

This balcony was once a special place to me, one of the sacred spots that children attach dreams to without knowing they are dreams.

It has a climbing morning-glory plant that winds

up one side of the railing, so that when you lean over there are purple-pink faces bobbing up and down on the vine. It is just right for eavesdropping on a game of hide and seek on a blowy day when blossoms are spun out of sight and whisked back again by the gamboling wind.

Then again, if one is a child, the daily ritual of hanging sheets over the rail—"to air them out," my grandmother used to say—seems a bit curious and imparts to the balcony, because of the bed trappings, the same aura of mystery and awesomeness that my grandparents' high bolstered bed had.

But the sheets fluttering in the breeze seemed so much more approachable, and there was a certain delight in watching the billows, and with a sudden reaching of my hand seeing them flatten again. On some days I was content to watch; on others I would construct a sailboat of the balcony, and use the blowing sheets for sails. There was something in the way the balcony hung over the yard, surrounded only by blue sky and puffs of clouds if I looked straight up, that gave it the bodiless, detached feel of moving craft. If I closed my eyes and felt only the flap of the sails against my face, and rocked slowly back and forth where I sat, I might have been undulating with the deep-sea movement of calm blue waters, or, on rougher days, I would strain and fight against the sharp surges of the gray and angry ocean.

Once in a while I would twist part of the sheet around the rail and let the rest cascade over me like a tent, and I would concoct all sorts of battle maneuvers for my troops, for I was nothing less than a general beneath the puffy white walls of my head-

quarters. Then in the midst of a great campaign I
felt the sides of the tent heave and collapse around
me as though it had been struck by cannon, and a
brief *thwack* struck the tent walls like a lone rifle
shot in a bold attack. Next thing I knew, I was
dangling in the air, sheet and all, my head peeping
shyly from a border of white, to meet my grandmother's frown, puffed from stooping, and to hear
her reprimand about trailing clean linen on the
ground. She would set me down and I would insist
on helping her shake the sheets in the breeze while
she tried halfheartedly to send me away. I helped
her fold the sheets, and we would stand a minute on
the balcony looking out, she with the sheets clutched
to her, and I pushing against her to see with her eyes
as well as my own. Then she would sigh and say
that if we looked far enough and half closed our
eyes against the glare, we would see beautiful things,
and she pointed my eyes to a thin figure in the distance, a monument, she said, of a famous general:
"See the horse up on his hind legs and the general's
arm up, as if to say 'forward.' He must have been an
important man, for they have built a whole park
around him, and they go to great trouble to have
flowers to match each season of the year. So it is not
a park that has been left to go, like some. Over to the
side, you can't see it from here, there is a huge fountain, with statues of strange creatures, half girl, half
fish, or half boy, half frog, and water shoots out of
their mouths, as though they were playing with each
other. In the middle is a very large turtle, oh very
wide—you could stretch out on him easily and trail
your finger in the water—but made of stone. It is a

grand park. We can almost see it from here."

I squinted and made out what must have been the general and his horse and some greenery; the rest I put there as my grandmother spoke. I never saw the park as a child. Only later, as a young man wandering about the city, did I see it, a rather formal place, I thought, tidy and well kept, but lacking that fantasy and wild naturalness I had imagined there below the general's feet from my perch on a far distant balcony.

That is a thing that happens with the years, no tragedy perhaps, but full of a vague disappointment. For as excited as a child must feel, only weeks old, to see a world unfolding around him, how less impressive must it be than the mist of color that surrounded him, with tints of yellow there, and a great splash of red before him. It is the same sense of disappointment that I felt on seeing the park, and today, stepping onto the balcony, my distress is greater, for former riches were there, dreams and fantasies and a true mist that covered the cracking concrete yard below, and a narrow alleyway beyond where garbage buckets line the curb and newspapers flutter in the street. And I can barely search out a church spire or the faint outline of a monument, for I cannot look beyond the houses which seem so close together, and the laundry next door deflects my gaze outward, and I have become myopic as well.

I close the door leading out to the balcony and am again in my grandparents' room, only my grandfather's now, which my mother keeps wonderfully clean and bright. There is the high bolstered bed and the tall chest with tiny drawers, and the heavy floor chest that holds the linens. They are the same, and, when searching for a place where I would be a stranger to no one, where could I go but here? For I have often felt that we are recognized by objects that have become familiar with our presence, and that have accepted our being there, for they strive to please us and to offer every other comfort. While still other times, there is a cool, unknowing stare thrust at us by everything we see, so much as to say we are unwanted company for which there is no appointed place; no space makes room for us and no niche stands waiting for us anywhere. We set it down as a stuffy place or a cold room or a tasteless one, which is just to say it has not accommodated itself to us or received us very well, or, in some cases, it may have rejected us altogether.

On the other hand, in some rooms, one can feel almost a part of the furniture, know it so intimately that any rearrangement or removal becomes a moment of personal discomfort or almost an act of maiming.

I have been familiar to my grandparents' room and have been made welcome by it. But there is something tired in it now, a weariness of saying hello or of putting itself out, so that I am still something of a stranger, even here, where if it were possible not to lapse into strangeness with the best-known things, it would certainly be so. Years away have intervened, and on return, one can sense the subterranean life that has gone on without us. We have no part in the alteration, or, more often still, we begin to detect the very surface of things we had grown too used to notice. I remember the start I had when we moved back to this old house from the Mulberry Street of Violet and Ann, and I laid my hand on the arm of the sofa. I withdrew it in surprise from the sharp encounter with the bristles, like the prickling of a thousand miniature barbs in the flesh. It was the same sofa where I was rocked as an infant, that I had leaped over as a child. Strange that I never noticed. . . .

But of all the familiar things, the strangest is to me the photograph that sits in a thin black frame on the high chest. It is the apotheosis of this room; the light from the balcony touches it in the morning, though for the most part it is set apart in the shade, off in a corner of the room where it can have a view of everything but see nothing.

It was the last photograph taken of my grandmother. Even that was two, perhaps three, years before her death, when her face was fuller and her eyes brighter than in the final days. Perhaps it is the face of the balcony days, looking far across the rooftops for the monument, or of the days when she would drop a tablespoon of coffee in my cup and fill the rest with milk on hot afternoons when the kitchen blinds were drawn, and the old ladies visiting waved fans made of painted palm back and forth as they spoke slowly and monotonously through the afternoon. There is a faint smile; she must have had happy memories she never spoke of. I covet them now when I remember only her sad eyes and the old tales of sickness and death that I heard from her—yes—when she herself was corroded with the evil worm that swelled with her sap and took her—petit marauder.

It is the strangest of all things—a photograph. Is the camera like some ancient mystic rite that lures its object into view, transfixes it with the peering lens, to entrap life there forever where it is eternally imprisoned in a spell? *Click* and it is done. Like the pale, blurred faces that had been in carnival booths where they drew the curtain closed: all was black, and *click,* they were painlessly impressed in the glass eye; only shades came out, clasping in their hands the changeling document.

I have before me all the old documents of my life —this photograph, this room, that all contain my life and other lives. . . . I will leave them for a while in mind and memory, to move now to places apart from these four walls, to the world outside my prison self, that is yet so everlastingly surrounded by the box shape of this doddering house, a mighty invisible frame, like the mysterious, omniscient curve of the round earth over us.

Part Two

(1)

IN OTHER days I turned all things into myself,
which was good in one way because it made me grow
fuller and taller; it gave me an eye to see, but in seeing, its object disappeared, absorbed into the great
repository that took things in, so that the outside was
outside no longer, but had become part of the inner
me. While there was a certain comfort in this transformation, there was with it a strange longing.

It was early in autumn when the leaves crackled
underfoot, some not yet dry enough to burn, others
spread out in brown clusters on the grass close by the
parent tree. Almost prematurely, they were cast onto
the growing pyre by a short dark man who capsized
the baskets of fallen leaves with the rapid, efficient
motion of his strong bare arms. I watched as he bent
to light them and then stepped back into the shadow
of trees to regard the fluctuating flame. Igniting easily, they burst at once into an ascending torch with
countless suppressed cries become one violent rustle
in the wind. A thin trail of smoke, all that was left
of the transformed leaves, moved over my head, becoming a thick arc of gray mist, with an odor star-

tlingly raw that brought a sharp pain to my senses. It seemed a thing unique, so incapable of occurring again that I wished the intake of experience to be redirected outward toward another, someone to know, too, the twinge of this exquisite aroma that verged on the unpleasant, and who, in the height of green summer, could summon up with me the lost moment of this autumn cremation.

Still suffused with the smell of burning leaves, I reached the classroom, sure the pungent fumes hung about me and somehow crept into my clothing to escape the annihilating dispersal into the open air.

I remember that day and that particular place of all the others—and, of course, Dr. Wengel, who sat at his desk, peering over a roomful of heads as he spoke, as though beyond us were another group to which he addressed himself, and beyond that still another. It had been his life's work so many decades by then that it undoubtedly appeared to him that only the faces changed, and in this he combined the characteristics of the teacher and the old man in equal portion, for he sought to stimulate anew what was essentially past.

He was somewhere between seventy and seventy-five and rumored to be retired each year. But he reappeared each fall for his weekly session, despite great physical impairment which caused him to walk painfully slow, feeling surfaces as he went. He had not lost, however, the great facility in speech that had marked his youth, nor the long, rhetorical phrases stylish in his time, nor the perennial exuberance of voice that was his professional asset. He was regarded with considerable humor and goodwill by the students as a kind of old-fashioned carry-over from another century, but with great deference, too, for his past reputation as teacher and scholar was well known.

It was that day that he had talked of dangerous currents of thought, and had finally looked directly at the group assembled before him to sum up. I remember that he bemoaned the failure of the philosopher in question to contribute positive ideas. He complained also of the residue of unsound speculation and insidious belief for which he was responsible, and which had had such a disastrous effect on our civilization. I can almost hear him finish with a flourish, almost giving the last syllables a drumroll with his tongue, and with this final cadence, rounding off the lecture to complement his opening remarks of the day. It meant that class was over. But before anyone could prepare to leave, there was an audible protest a few seats from me and the tumult of a body roused to its feet in indignation. Everyone turned to stare at the unusually tall figure in the aisle, blond hair rising out of long, thin face. A few smiles were exchanged and someone mumbled, "It's Richter again." I heard the crisp, slightly exasperated voice that commanded everyone's attention.

"Is every man responsible, then, for what becomes of his ideas in the hands of those who twist them to their own purpose?"

Dr. Wengel looked at the student in the back row, who stood frowning with unblinking eyes, holding his firm jaw tightly in, awaiting an answer. Then he replied in his measured speech, "Yes—yes, Mr. Richter, I think so."

"But then invention can be written off at the outset." The student looked as though he might approach the desk at any moment and punctuate the remarks on the desk top. Then one saw it was the intensification of the eyes that seemed to animate every other particular. The rest of his person remained immobile, and it was the alarming dominance of the eyes that gesticulated, intruded, pounded tables in its stead. The words followed one another just as precisely, but with more vigor and conviction than before.

"No man can freely speculate with one eye on posterity and the other on possible consequences were he misunderstood." His head bobbed slightly now with his excitement, but his hair remained undisturbed, neatly groomed; in fact, one could see how strokes of the brush had made divisions of the hair, sending one force straight back, others off to the side, one around the curve of the ear. It was that genus of blond hair ridden with shadow that lifted the blondness to the very fore. By this time, he was wildly waving his hands in the air.

"He must take the risk, knowing that his idea—because it is bold and revolutionary and apt to appeal to restless minds—may, for these reasons, fall into the very hands of those most unprepared for them." His increasing intensity was in marked contrast to the impatience around him. "His responsibility is to his idea, not to what is done with it."

"You speak of invention, Mr. Richter, but what is that, after all? I would suppose the really most original thoughts were those that agitated the demented mind, but I am just as happy to have that originality contained. You forget that there is such a thing as the morality of an idea, of a thing being implicitly moral or immoral. It is here that the choice is made, that its consequences are weighed. And here the responsibility begins."

"I don't believe ideas are moral or immoral. I would hold each man responsible for what he makes of an idea. At its origin, I would concern myself only with the brilliance of the insight, the consistency of its logic, and the soundness of its argument. Then the philosopher is done with his responsibility."

"Ah yes—its internal logic and applications." Here Dr. Wengel paused, and a familiar semi-smile appeared, the same that his students had all come to recognize as the "Stermer" smile, for when he began to recount stories of those old days or to think of them, this same half-smile would engage his face. Many came to Wengel's class for just these outbursts of reverie surrounding the leading philosopher of the day, and it was curious to think this man had been his teacher, and was still active in the classroom in a time when he could see in ascendance the arguments he had tried to counter decades before in their early state, when their youthful founder was but a student in his class. He regarded this with considerable irony rather than with essential bitterness, his final lecture in the course, devoted to the philosophy of Stermer, becoming thereby legendary with the students.

"That would not at all surprise me on other lips as well—but then, you all seem to think that way automatically these days. It may be that Stermer had great insight into the modern mind before it knew

itself— That may be it, after all— However—oh
yes, by doing away with the moral point of view, Mr.
Richter, I take it you relinquish the necessity of God,
the belief in meaningful existence? But how is it
possible, then, to structure the universe? That is, it
seems to me, what philosophy is largely about. What
is to keep one from admitting all possibilities equally,
including destruction itself?"

"But who can deny that?" Richter burst out. "It is
the only means we have to creation and understanding. Certainly, if there were a creator, he knew this
very well, if we take his word as evidence. Didn't he
destroy darkness to create light and the infinite to
form time? Every created thing is infused with the
prospect of its own destruction—death. If we must
judge the morality of ideas by their potential destruc-
tiveness, we must throw out the whole lot of them.
An idea begins by destroying what was thought before it."

Dr. Wengel's underlying ironies had changed
slowly to a contained anger. "We have gone quite
far enough, Mr. Richter, and very far afield. We are
discussing a philosophy that has elevated the individual above moral law, and that has replaced universal
considerations with particular ones. I thought that
fifty years of war and revolution resulting from this
point of view would have convinced everyone of
its invalidity, even of its immorality, by now!" He
paused to take a breath, and the short interval cooled
him. He seemed to reflect on other times for a moment before continuing, and his gaze was kinder.

"So many of you have imbibed that particular spirit
of destroying foundations, of looking with a hard eye

on any metaphysical idea, and examining everything through the scrutiny of signs and symbols. And yet, I can imagine Stermer now, laughing uproariously at being taken at his word. I remember a long time ago—it will be thirty years soon, and none of you can know what that means, not even having lived that long—but that long ago Eric and I sat by the window of that coffee shop across the way. It was right there by the window that we had our frankest talk, as though we were not a whole generation removed, and he not a student at all. I told him he couldn't possibly believe his own arguments. The idea seemed to put him into a rage, and I prepared myself for his fist-pounding on the table. . . . He was a great fist-pounder in his day. . . . You remind me of him a great deal, Mr. Richter. . . . But there was no banging and no rage that day. He stopped himself short, and burst, instead, into an uncontrollable laugh." Dr. Wengel sucked in his breath. "What we used to call the demonic . . . but it is as modern as any of you . . . that terrible, bloodless laughter— And I knew then that it would not pass over with Eric as I had thought it would. I tried to say so much then, but how does one say the kind of thing I meant? . . . Somehow I always see him that way first—and in the classroom after that—this very classroom where I introduced him to those dangerous currents he has fashioned into a school." The semi-smile and the far-away look were fading. "But where have we wandered to from your first question, Mr. Richter? And it is past time already."

With that, Dr. Wengel gathered together his notes, and the class dispersed with the first rising of his ponderous body. Richter sat stiffly in his seat with the frustration of an unfinished argument plainly on his face. I could not help feeling a great sympathy for his stubborn mind as I stood watching him, but I was nonetheless surprised to hear myself speak out suddenly.

"It was a good argument from your end—well taken and well stated."

He looked up at me, for the first time aware someone was there, shading his eyes as he looked toward the light, weighing my sincerity.

"He carries on an argument like an idiot." A touch of boyishness crept over the sophistication, and having said this, he seemed less irritated and took up his books. Without exchanging another word with me, he fell into step by my side, as though it were the most natural thing in the world that we should leave together and continue our conversation in a new atmosphere.

How difficult to summon a place such as the university, a collective place, one where so many experiences and impressions cancel one another in memory! Except that the evocation of the coffee shop and the memory of myself at its window illumines the abstraction, so that recalling the one brings the other automatically into focus and I know again what it was to be there.

Tables were set exactly at the window ledge, and only glass divided the whole outside from the clusters of tables safely tucked within. Sitting there, I witnessed the procession of figures idling past, the jostle of people hurrying to get where they were

going, the tangle of arms and legs moving freely in
all directions. The coffee shop and the transient
groups might have occurred anywhere, but as the
groups thinned, they were placed in only this milieu
by the tall, monarchial buildings that emerged beyond, some just across the street, others farther still,
each belying its separateness, insisting on its revered
place as part of a larger whole. For the first time I
had a sense of this allegiance that bound those dissimilar, incongruous shapes, making common fealty.
From the window I could watch the squat, brown
building opposite, where Wengel's class had ended
and from which I had just emerged with the silent,
hunched figure beside me. Next to it was the red-
brick library Richter had laughingly called Washing-
ton's Headquarters, and an imposing gray building
farther off, the Theater Hall, with the grim ex-
terior of a mausoleum but more lively than any other
place on the campus. Then we had crossed the street
and taken this place at the window, looking out of
it at the buildings, with our separate thoughts. I wondered if Dr. Wengel had sat where we sat, with the
university staring at him . . . Stermer beside him,
thinking the old man part of that grand allegiance
they both faced.

There was a clatter in the coffee shop—cups and
spoons rattling, the blur of voices, and music filtering through now and then. Amid all those fuzzy
sounds, Richter's voice had a contrasting clarity and
definiteness. Its sharp, incisive quality struck me all
the more at the small table where we sat than it
had in the expanses of the classroom.

"I was thinking of Wengel in this place."

I nodded as he continued, "Thirty years ago! I wonder if someone like Wengel could ever have been a young revolutionary once."

"That's always hard to tell. In thirty years' time people can become pretty hard to recognize, even to themselves."

I remembered a certain Midsummer Night and sighed before returning to the subject at hand. "There must be many a reformed rebel hiding beneath layers of wrinkles and new flesh."

"Oh yes." Richter seemed somewhat impatient, but I realized, even on such short acquaintance, that it was a mannerism he had, not intended to reflect a particular mood. "There's no denying that. I wonder, though, if most people were ever much different from the present day. Usually they have only reached at middle age what they embraced long, long before."

"Still, it's a grisly business—growing old. I can imagine someone not the least bit staid or satisfied wanting in those last years to have things pretty much close circle, round themselves off. He wants to be able to look back on his life as a totality before he dies."

"Yes." Richter seemed pleased with the idea, seizing it eagerly, developing it in swift, deft strokes as he spoke.

"I suppose we can't really blame him for that. You and I, young people in general, can live with all the fragments that don't fall into place, hoping they will somehow, sometime. There is enough time to wait and see. But the old can't trust to hope and time to form the unity. So each imposes a different order to make the fragments congeal into a life. Oh yes, I can sympathize entirely."

"Who is to say that it's wrong? Some may have battled a long time before reaching for that way of ordering, that fitting things into place."

He smiled a little ironically. "Something happens to them." He paused and fixed his eye on me with a great intensity, so that one felt one ought to grip something, and I pressed tightly on my cup, the side of the table, any *physical* thing. "Life happens to them. Life that keeps changing and won't stop when they're ready to settle with what they've got." His voice softened to a surprising sympathetic note. "It won't stop and *they* will. So they must catch up what they can. . . ."

His voice trailed off, and the rising clatter in the room resumed its former pre-eminent place. New faces appeared on all sides, and outside the procession of figures continued to stream past the window. It had not slackened while we talked; only we had stopped taking notice of it.

Glancing back at Richter, I saw his mouth frame the word "change" without a sound accompanying it. It was not part of the conversation, but his thought processes flying to his lips, a lapse common to those more versed in introspection than in dialogue. I knew it well. He caught my unintentional smile and, half embarrassed, shared with me the thought that might otherwise have passed from one part of him to another in incestuous silence.

"I can't help thinking of that wonderful moment . . . perhaps it was a whole lifetime in the making . . . when Heraclitus looked into a river and saw the passing of all life there. How it passed by in all its variety, and could never be the same in the next moment as it had been in the preceding one . . . never *quite* the same." He paused. There seemed something magical in the words he had just spoken. "It takes a grandeur to see that, courage to accept. Perhaps, if we have it in us not to weaken, we will know it like that, too."

We were both silent and thoughtful, and neither of us felt inclined to speak after that.

We got up to leave, and only at the door did we see that tiny drops of rain were falling, swelling into great splotches on the sidewalk. As it happened, we were going in opposite directions and said good-bye in the doorway before launching our separate assaults into the rain. Richter began to run just ahead of the drops; they seemed to pelt him lightly from behind until he grew dim and out of focus, lost to my eyes in the haze of rain blown with increasing force across the darkened street.

My room that night was very still, and I was especially silent. When I walked, or changed position in my chair, the sound seemed tuned up, magnified by some invisible current. I had to set aside the book I read because each page seemed a symmetrical design of ink smudges, and I could not get any of them to articulate as sounds in my mind. When I tried to think, it seemed I went over the same phrases again and again; then I saw that it was my whole habit of mind that had not moved from its set place; everything about my thoughts, my voice, my room seemed inbred and familiar.

And with this feeling of irritation at the room, I sought to feel its presence. Yes, these too had become familiar things, but unlike beloved objects in that other room of old, they stood aloof and comfortless. They were not invested with the further shape that years and intimacy mold atop an outer form. This room, in contrast, was vague, anonymous, dull as most college rooms are dull, stripped to the bleak essential, barren of identity. In such a room, it was I who must impart to it a character, overflow into the room something of myself, impinge on chairs and desk, on couch and bed, on all those bland, assorted, unparticular things, some striking sense that had the touch of me. It was, unlike the warmth of womb and nest made ready for our refuge, the cool outside that we must warm ourselves.

I remembered the specialness that surged to mind at thought of faded blue, the armchair that held aloft from shipwreck in the night, an old man's dehydrated form, supporting its sudden stir when close to fearful sleep, his vigilant limbs contracting at thought that it might be their last awaking. In contrast, this armchair where I sat, flowered in haste, turned a blank face into the room. I had conveyed nothing to it nor it to me, though I could feel without the looking for my mark on its familiar hulk. There, where my fingers rested, were two holes where the long ash of midnight cigarettes had fallen, sinking far into the soft earth of the chair arm where it had spawned these two white blossoms that curled into my fingers at the slightest touch.

What else was there of me? Books were scattered throughout the room, the old piled high into corner

heaps; current interests, that might testify in my behalf, were invisible to view, slipped as they were at
night beneath the bed, where I grew sleepy as I read.
No, I had not added a rug or pillow, not a picture on
the wall. All was as I had found it. Even the hot
plate, its dull surface watchful in its corner, had been
there before, left unwanted by its past owner who
rejected the prolonged agonies of its warming that I
accepted, awaiting its tardy fire without even the
small impatience I might indulge myself.

Such thoughts recalled the couch in our old house
—how it rose a stranger to my fingertips with the
slightest distance. Then, that distance was of time—
a hiatus in our everyday. Now, there was no breaking
of the flow of time. The distance was made visible
by my searching—the distance of that unperceived,
wide physical space that separated the room and me.
I saw the gap.

The events that day had stirred in me a deep dissatisfaction with the way things were, and made the
long chain of solitary days that stretched before me
a dreary and distasteful future; yet I saw where they
had stretched into the past behind me, and it had
seemed a natural succession I had not even thought
to question. Now I felt they could never occur in the
way they or I fully expected, for it was possible to
uproot the waiting days, and fill them with sounds
and thoughts undreamed of by the inseeking world
where I lived days of habit and accustomed silence.

With the heat of former pride now turned to
shame, I remembered the dialogues with Michael,
happy then that I could sustain his existence as well
as my own, that there was a perpetual overflow in

me so that the small boy who began when I began
need not be annihilated while I had means to maintain him. It seemed ingenious and easy then, but,
expanding, I had begun to exhaust those inner resources by which we grow for a while almost of ourselves and rely on little outside to feed us. Less and
less could be spared as I engulfed the world, ingest-
ing it with unending appetite. It was insufficient now
even for myself, for my dissatisfaction had become
more acute. Now there was this Richter, and I marveled at the nearness of a mind completely outside
my being, over which I had no control and no vital
connection. That was what was remarkable. He there
and I here, yet surely there was a means to cross over,
one to the other. How, I could not imagine, nor what
to do from my end to extend a bridge. It even seemed
a little farfetched. I had always been convinced that
people were ultimately solitary—apartness was the
natural, inevitable state—and that had served me well
enough in the past. This tentative reaching out, even
in my thoughts, might be foolish fancy, sure to prove
embarrassing, impossible, or both.

But still, something of me sought a link, drawing
me out toward the strangeness the words "Phil Richter" represented. Perhaps something in him seemed
vaguely familiar, enough like me to be recognizable,
or, if not quite that, an embodiment of things, not
fully expressed, toward which I groped. If so, he was,
in a way, an extension of myself. I wondered, had
things been otherwise, if I might not almost have
been in Phil Richter's place, able to talk as he did,
with that clear, incisive quality of voice, a little exasperated with the world—whatever it was that seemed

to set him off so definitely from his fellows. It seemed a distinct possibility, one of the things that *might* have happened to one but didn't; for hadn't a small boy been thwarted from the church aisle by some unbidden choice that carried him instead in an unforeseen swirl through the carnival world? Wasn't it only one of many possibilities we become, this and not that, for no apparent reason, whatever postulation we put forward only posing a fresh question? Might there not be, out of all those possible ways, one to carry us so far from the place it started that it is another life altogether, Phil Richter's perhaps and not mine at all?

But wait—I had almost been tricked by my unwilling mind, still trying to turn everything in upon itself, even this new experience, for it had succeeded so long in claiming the outside world as part of its own diverse inner being. It was this way of thought from which I sought release, for though there might be many possibilities, this was the one that *was* at the present moment. Only one had *happened,* and it was this one that lay awake musing in a quiet room, this one that could think *about* Phil Richter without being him. I could almost see a procession of shadows in my mind, faceless all of them, shades that stood dumbly watching me, with a touch of the forlorn about them, as though but for ever so little, *they* could have been, too.

Through all of these wakeful and unquiet thoughts, I felt something rising in me, restlessly darting from one place to another, gathering flame in its press upward, becoming frenzied in its search for a means to escape when every way seemed barred to it; imprisoned, it burned to a searing whiteness beyond heat or light, painfully intense. It might have come from a place unknown to me, where it could gather fire in secret and dart out already raging and full of its sudden, sharp pain. At its height I felt a wave of suffocation and was left covered with moisture.

Why should loneliness assault me on this day of all days, when it seemed paradoxically at an end, when there was almost a certainty of having found what had eluded me all the years? Somewhere back where I couldn't see it clearly, I realized that something very extraordinary, taken for granted by the rest of the world, could go on around me. It was possible for people to sense something of one another as they talked, for them to catch a little of another's deeper humanity in a brief exchange, and walls of twos and threes could spring up, unforeseen, in place of a solitary structure. I had never fully known the sense of incompleteness that I felt in the dark unknown place I spoke of, and the longing that had burst into fire there for someone completely apart from me whom I could know with a certainty, as I sometimes knew myself. And here was Richter, this person who had suddenly presented himself and forced upon me a true knowledge of another existence, a realization that was strong and sharp enough to make a careful solitary wall crumble with the white fire of its aloneness.

It had to be a thing of the most enormous power to steal from me that solitude some men search for a lifetime and never find. But I do not underestimate its grip nor the strength of its aroused body stirring.

For it is a sleeping giant, and we never know when it is awake until it has come into the house, leaving the fences torn behind it, and it strides upon us from out of nowhere, wrenching from us the possibility of escape by its very presence. It overpowers because it is *there,* because it was *always* there and we, unsuspecting that this great, towering, omnipotent tyrant existed at all, let alone in the very environs of our being, where it can resuscitate itself at will to half crush out the life in us—and we unequal to the combat.

Loneliness!—I can breathe it now that you have gone to rest and I dare summon the shouts and blows you withered with your breath! Can anyone who has known you hear my cries with equanimity, knowing he too may be at your mercy, even in the next moment when you were nowhere, and now suddenly appear and are a strong hand straining at his throat? Loneliness!—terrible phoenix, you fade with a fierce smile, knowing you will rise the stronger for your deceptive death, ever ready for pursuit, and we your victims and your prey so long as we have breath and live!

That first fearful knowledge endures; it survives for me still. That night is impressed on my memory as the loneliest I ever spent. It was the night the possibility of *not* being lonely presented itself for the first time.

(2)

WHEN my friend and I visited St. Anne de Beaupré, we had detoured on a vacation trip to make this pilgrimage. My waning zeal and Phil's amused superiority led us to that place, dreams of impregnable monastery walls high above the sea, salt rocks below, a view of infinite sea and sky beyond. We saw a minor cathedral, landlocked, not even facing the sea. Where we had imagined black cassocks, even cowls against the damp wind, and fringed shawls on gaunt pilgrim women who moved parched lips to say the rosary, were tourist faces we had left smiling in camera poses in upper Quebec.

The desperate fervor that had erected the first monument at that site was surely absent, as was a roughhewn character, an old-sea-ship look, that grateful Breton sailors would have carved into the stone and worked into the plaster. Once this was a pledge gift to the mother saint who plucked a doomed craft from the sea and tucked it on the shore, Beaupré. Now on that site someone had built this grand cathedral, a collection of small buildings for one enterprise or other, circular, rectangular, flat modern storefront—none the stark tribute of the sailors, with simple, strong lines against the sea.

We wondered how the Old World had, to all appearances, survived, while the New World seemed always to obscure her past in rebuilding. The original

stones, rock, plaster, spirit seemed to endure centuries
of Sinai sand and wind, Roman sun and rain, Gallic
seas and wars, whereas the New World swallowed
her small history as a guppy gulps her young. Yearly,
old churches, houses, relics are devoured by fire, by
flood, by civic improvement, and by complete re-
modeling enterprises. There seemed such little sense
of history, such persecution of it to serve the whim
of currency, even in Quebec where unseen forces
strained to keep the old intact, but slowly failed.

At St. Anne de Beaupré few pilgrims rubbed the
dark earth with their knees to ascend the sacred
slope. More often they looked about as they had on
many another tour, and spent most of their time in
the mission shop, in the familiar atmosphere of sou-
venir corners. The favorite when we visited were tiny
bottles for holy water that sold for a small fee. We
would have liked to laugh at our disappointment,
and to tell the truth, we made many jokes about the
hard, pious faces that entered the cathedral, and came
out, seconds later, gleaming for the bargain counter.
But with all our jokes, we felt a momentary bleak-
ness that pilgrimages were no longer possible. The
priests were too well-fed without enjoying what they
ate with that full, hearty appreciation old ribald friars
had had. And our modern pilgrims—if they made a
pledge or vowed a march, it was such a dreary, trying, vexing thing unless they made of it a touring
ground and vacation trip. For if *we* did not believe,
we had thought that there was a devotion somewhere
that Italian masters had drawn from, and that this
spirit was what would last forever, if all the rites were
ended and if the paintings cracked into pieces. Where

was the sea-spray, and in the grotto of St. Anne, where were the rotted oars? There was neither faith in the pilgrims nor truth in the symbol. Yet we were sure that we could stand a whole day before *one* Michelangelo fresco and know all the grandeur there was in religion and the power that could be faith.

This was how we spoke to each other, Phil and I, as though our impressions were seen as one, as if the intervening wall of our nervous systems had become transparent and the effort of relaying messages, wearying and inaccurate, had been dispensed with. So it was no wonder that several times I stopped myself in midsentence to find we had both spoken at once and were saying very nearly the same things. Only on such occasions it was always Phil who plunged ahead to complete the thought, and I who fell back, for he was under the greater press of a rapid, over-agile mind, and restraint came more easily to me. Other times a bystander, hearing our argument, would have grown bewildered by a logic that skipped stages as ours did, by that unspoken mutual consent that persists in conversations between close friends. But with Phil this was carried further than in most friendships, so even I, an initiate, had sometimes to strain for the connection, catch up, so to speak, in my own mind to where he had thrust the line of argument. I preferred this stretching to the adventure on my part to a retrieving action on his, and, too, it was probably these very unnegotiated terms that made our relationship so satisfactory to him and so beneficial to me.

It was that rare time in friendship when we left ourselves unguarded from each other, so that our impressions and sensations emerged unfiltered, un-refined, with a strength and energy that tapped a reserve of power unsuspected by either of us. Our exchanges generated ideas and subtleties of intellect that had never appeared before, so that each mind sought the other to reach the mountain fastnesses, the recesses, and the headwaters which we separately contained. But most of all we laughed, turning into humor our loneliest thoughts and our truest aspirations. Our friendship had to be taken out-of-doors and aired a bit, made tougher by the exasperating heat of the sun and the sudden coolness of evening. For, as we drove south from Canada, this was the coastland in summer—that summer and every summer, I suppose—dry and thirsty and happy to abandon itself to extremes of temperature when the punitive sun went down.

Sometimes in our wanderings we kept to the highways, but their unrelieved symmetries became so tiresome that we would welcome any promising offshoots with uneven, tree-tipped roads and a peculiar forest fragrance. There were long stretches of road when there was little to say and few words passed between us, when we were content to muse with the unpeopled farmland that rolled under us or to aspire with the sides of mountains that pushed themselves upward with lonely effort. Other times we became so excited with our talk that we could barely drive on, and many a country curve was taken with arms flailing the air in argument and eyes rapt in the course of discussion.

Once when we saw an opening in the trees, we could sense at once the coolness of the water-soaked air, and knew without a further sign that a mountain stream had wound its way among the giant trees and pressed itself ever more deeply into the yielding forest bed. Hot from the dusty road, we looked in awe at the clear mountain water that still preserved in its chill glitter its former snowflake essence.

With short yelps we pushed ourselves into the water and were revived by the first splash of it into our faces. Our indolent bodies began performing vigorous spirals and effortless arcs through air and water, until the initial mineral spirits subsided and we lolled, half floating on the surface. That immeasurable calm spoken of water lifted us to a horizontal plane, so that we were unsinkable even on the miniature crests that pressed up under us. Without any effort on our part we remained suspended, and it seemed nothing existed but the changeless sky overhead and the cool rippling life that seeped out of us into the eddying stream. Blinking, we turned our eyes from the sky, and saw passing on the bank sudden patches of brown and green, and our joint gaze was arrested a longer moment by a grotto of stone and a black-draped figure with raised fingers—the Black Virgin of the Rocks that Canadian farmers placed everywhere to invoke a blessing—and that looked ineffectual and helpless as she tried in vain to stay the river and to keep us rooted by her side. I turned my head and half my body to look back at her again, and in so doing I toppled and was suddenly upright in the tugging current, every tree and rock a clear entity bathed in sunlight, and now turning on his stomach in the water was Phil, almost beside me, where he, too, had been carried by the water.

I looked at him and saw passing from his eyes the sweet immobility we had felt together, and I knew as our gaze met quietly that we had experienced not only the same moment but almost the same thoughts. The water that lapped against my chest lapped also against Phil, and its transparent touch was broken by the sunlit outline of his flesh as by mine. We had both been held suspended on the face of the water by a bond of oversky and undersea that kept us afloat and bodiless together for a timeless space. It was a thing experienced in common, not he through me, nor I through him; in our separate worlds we had been touched by the same purgative mineral spring that sustained us while we let drop our human form, while it ran down into the chill whiteness and reluctantly returned to restore time and place, vision and thought into that reciprocal gaze by which we recognized each other and saw how closely persons might be joined by their blind nonhuman selves. As I reflected on it, Phil pushed himself forward, and feet up, threw splotches of water on me, breaking the even pattern of the stream into a shimmering and impermanent design.

(3)

CONSIDER the stage. There is the actor and then the role he plays, two separate entities that join within an evening to become a single life. A feat commonly enough performed, it still, to my mind, remains an extraordinary event.

Suppose the actor were a known friend, and having seen him only hours before, I was now confronted with his dramatic presence. Would I distinguish him beneath the layers that obliterated his daily face, make out the friend I knew despite the unfamiliar grimace, the peculiar accent he had assumed? Would something in the voice recall him, some known gesture he was not aware of making spirit him back upon the stage when I had thought him banished for the evening? Worse still, might not an actor at some point recollect himself, suddenly unarch the back bent to make him old, feel the heavy lines impressed upon his face, and wonder why he spoke in such an artful way, a strained cover upon the voice? Perhaps a gesture of his own might intrude itself upon the character he had become, arousing a momentary confusion that sets him suddenly within a room of strangers, in dress appropriate to another time, another place, wondering why so many eyes had settled upon him as though he were about to speak. Is this unfortunate consciousness of self the demon that steals upon the stage bearing lapses of memory, distortions of line in the wake of premature revival?

Conversely, might not an actor become so at one with his stage role that he is incapable of withdrawing from it at all? Surely there are some who retain that image of the stage beyond its setting, and who with difficulty find again the tone and gesture that heralds the natural self temporarily exiled from existence. Consider the barely conceivable intricacy of impersonation in certain plays of Shakespeare, where the actor is asked to play a role within a role, super-impose upon the original an assumed identity to be sustained within the play, maintaining beneath them both his own person that waits to be resumed. How does he keep them separate, the King in *A Winter's Tale,* the Visitor he disguises himself to be, and the player who flings aside both velvet mantle and pilgrim's cloak to wear his street clothes out into the night?

These were not thoughts one has amid the everyday. But seated in a theater facing the stage it came quite naturally, this speculation on those layers of illusion that unfold there before one's very eyes. It was my first evening within the Theater Hall that I passed each day. There in my seat at its very center, I felt more involved than ever before in that experience it laid before any who would receive it. Between the acts my mind was stirred by questions the author asked in his players' guise. Once he moved his spokesman upon the stage before a mirror, had him confront that quizzical reflection with his own Pirandellian smile, and ask the silent image, which was real —what looked into the mirror or what looked back? His finger pointed into the glass at his reflection, but there it directed itself again to him. The impasse of those facing fingers remained in view long after that brief dramatic moment was eclipsed by others.

I joined wholeheartedly in the applause and went backstage with Phil at the end of the performance. He had become friendly with several members of the group, particularly with a girl who had been a leading player that night. He passed from one to another of them, shaking their hands vigorously, combining

with his praise some critical remarks which I could
only guess at from his habit of staring intently, followed by a screwing up of the eyes. I could surmise
the nature of what was being said from where I stood
off to one side to avoid the steady stream of people who clustered around the actors, making their
extravagant speeches. I had begun myself to look
around at what now lay exposed to view. What had
seemed an unblemished surface of solid blue from my
seat below, I now saw to be a fine speckling on every
wall, all those dots and flecks of paint combining
from a distance to form a solidity not there in fact.
And, too, I saw supports behind each wall, arms that
reached to hold the room in place, which from outside, those hours of the play, had seemed so sturdy
and solid a chamber that I had felt myself within as
pleasant and comfortable a sitting room as I had ever
seen.

A peculiar cosmetic film hung in the air, imposing
itself upon senses unused to its sharp presence, much
as the odor of turpentine assaults the stranger upon
entering, those first moments, the painter's world.
Before my eyes, players were wiping color from their
smudged faces, obliterating with hurried, deft strokes
the characters that had been created for the stage.
One actress had already removed her make-up and
stood laughing with her own ordinary face protrud-
ing from the wide collar and flecked aqua print that
had projected so well the upper-class gentility of a
small town. The combination of her pert, modern
head and this provincial dress in the already disman-
tled room had a grotesque quality, reminding one of
those old-fashioned comic photographs, where some-

one had posed, for its incongruous charm, behind the ruffled neck of period costume. On another side I was attracted by the special inflection of a voice, distinguishable even in its present lightness and banter as that of the tortured son-in-law of the play. Seeing the face from which it came, I thought the similarity coincidental, for the young man standing there had too much nose and mouth to recall the character of the stage, yet my eyes would not budge from those heavy, puffed lips from which came that distorted but unmistakably familiar sound. Beyond him, talking quietly with someone, was still another player, half her face swathed in lines and wrinkles of old age, the other wiped clean of make-up, the ridge of her nose dividing sharply the skin severely white and smooth in contrast to the dark powders of the stage. With her hand she scooped the cold cream that in a moment would erase all traces of her past existence. While she held it poised in air, Phil came, leading me in some excitement to the first-night party being given nearby.

The party was in a large house full of people I had never met. No host in sight, already crowded, it was the kind of party at which every newcomer made his way, mixing with other guests or retreating, according to his social whim. At first I pushed along the crowds with Phil but lost him soon after we arrived. Across the room I saw him bending slightly over Connie, whom I had never met but had heard mentioned several times before he greeted her backstage. They made a striking couple, both tall, he blond, dark-eyed, intense, she solidly earthbound, naturally ruddy of cheek and lips, with thick, honey-colored hair wound intriguingly to crown the head. She brought to mind the slopes of Thuringia or the broad fields of the Ukraine, arousing by her presence incisive, long-forgotten smells of country summers, a mixture of cut grain and apples ripening on trees. Overflowing with good spirits, she kept Phil amused and in excellent humor the evening long. I saw their tall heads weaving in and out, bobbing up and down according to the loftiness of their surroundings, until gradually I lost them in the crowd of new faces that kept appearing in a never ending stream from the hallway. I took part in several conversations which had drawn me casually into a shifting group, for there was constantly a recombination and reshuffling of people that kept the room in constant flux, guests winding their way from one small gathering to another, to and from the refreshment table. Once or twice I approached a familiar face, but intercepting a bewildered, unrecognizing stare before I spoke, I moved on, embarrassed to realize it was someone from the play whom I had mistaken, because of that brief intimacy of the stage, for an acquaintance.

It puzzled me that all the players were so quick to drop the mood and aspect of the play, almost as though the experience of early evening had not occurred. Reflecting on it, I stepped back, not thinking anyone behind me, inadvertently pushing against the wall someone who gave a startled sound, half smothered by the bit of cake so recently placed between the lips. Unlike others at their ease in those surroundings, she seemed out of her element, all the more constrained because my clumsiness had forced me upon the retreat she had fashioned of this corner. To re-

assure her, I smiled into the startled eyes she turned
on mine. All through them, particularly in the inmost circle of her gaze, hung a familiar look, that
recent voiceless protest of the eyes that reached across
the stage each time the mother of the Pirandello play
appeared. Though the lines were erased from her face
and the white brushed from her hair, only these ap-
purtenances had disappeared when she had wiped
away that former guise. Beneath it, existing without
external form, she had retained the agonized intensity
of her role. While I apologized once again for clumsy
jostling, my thoughts merged with my words, and
unaware until I did it, I called her by that name by
which I knew her: Signora Frola. Her face cleared of
the strained, self-conscious look a moment, and she
smiled. I noticed then the severe whiteness of her
skin, and recalled that I had seen that face before.
Yes, just one side white, piquant like this, free of the
lines and wrinkles still covering that darker profile—
she who had the cold cream gathered on the fingertips, ready to erase all evidence of that protesting
Signora Frola who, as I left, remained still partially
intact.

With almost a stammer I commented on the mysterious quality she brought onto the stage, exactly
right for the enigmatic figure she had portrayed.
Again she smiled, seizing on what I said as though
all the evening she had been waiting for someone to
discuss the play with her beyond congratulation, as
though all else were empty praise and now at last she
could unburden herself to someone who, like her,
had still one foot within the drama, had not quite
left the Theater Hall. Together we drifted to an-

other corner where we could talk. I watched her eyes flicker with excitement in speaking of her role and the important unresolved quality of the play. An enormous sigh came as she spoke of the strange, veiled heroine who appeared in the final scene.

". . . a phantom who chose to be both this and that . . . because she was no one," she ended with her heavy sigh.

"Not just *one*." I could not help correcting her remark, remembering my own strong sense of dualness about the role.

"No," Laura insisted softly with an emphasis that left no room for quarrel, *"no one."* She smiled again, pulling her lips back to show the barest whiteness of teeth. Thus with becoming stubbornness she closed the first phase of our talk, and I, accompanied by that quiet echo, so recent an acquisition, left to gather more refreshments.

From across the room I watched her a long moment, needing this farther distance to clearly perceive her. She still sat formally erect, her lovely, translucent face strained, not quite relaxed in summoning motions appropriate to social ease. In her exposed position, alone, more people stopped to greet her, and she complied uneasily, as though some sense of oughtness kept her there. Perhaps in the renewed burst of social discourse she recalled how our rapt conversation had shielded her from just this obligation. For from where I stood I watched how she turned to search, almost in some distress, for my return and then faintly smile, relieved, when I stepped forward, as though merely my approach had effected a welcome rescue.

The evening ended with our walking the short distance to her home. The chill early winter was in the air and the sky was black from the distant sun. One's eyes were drawn upward as they are on clear, dark nights when there is silence between walkers.

We talked of many things, each trying gently to pry open doors to the other's inner world. A sympathy coursed between us, and in our tentative remarks and groping questions we tried, without knowing how, to explain the particularity that was that night.

"Why are there so many stars—so many more than usual?" She asked as though the uniqueness that we felt might lie in that.

"Yes, it can grow crowded up there on clear nights."

Her head was already turning to different places along the dotted-swiss blackness of the sky.

"I think I see Orion." With her head tilted back, the dark wave of her hair slipped farther down the neck. I withdrew my gaze reluctantly to follow the figure she traced broadly with agile fingers. "We learned them all in school, but now I find only one or two that I remember."

"What about *them?*—Over there, just beyond his club . . . those two bright lights together. . . ." She hesitated.

"Castor and Pollux," I prodded, and this time she followed the motion of my finger gliding through air, joining their bodies, showing their heads.

"Oh, Gemini, the twins." She was pleased to have remembered and smiled shyly, her face brightening, gently transformed by the touch of even a small satisfaction.

"Yes, Gemini." I smiled my secret affinity for those stars, which, in my childhood, had stirred me to nocturnal searches for just those two immortal heads, lifting them, with the peculiar significance I attached to their presence, out of all the stars of the sky. They were still etched there, though I had not looked for them in years, perhaps a decade. Now, not having spoken it before, I found thought of that private realm filtering cautiously through to her, but under great restraint of our strangeness to each other. I though it might have been the stars, the involuntary pull of the dark heavens that stirred lost dreams, dark memories, and reawakened early wonder, glamour I had found in picking out those luminous lights from all the sweep of sky.

"Those two—" I was still pointing—"I know very well. On the balcony where we lived I watched them all the time. Sometimes they seemed far off and I could barely pick them out. But then, some days they came down close, like now, and jumped out from the sky. I could see them exactly, to the very faces, as I had seen them traced in a book once . . . 'The Heavenly Twins' it said, and underneath it told their story. That was years and years ago."

"Then tell me, too." She glimpsed the closeness that was passing behind façades of words and watched intently that tiny space of stars. "I know nothing beyond the names."

It was hard to understand how anyone who spoke as quietly as she, giving the words a warm turn with her dark voice, could move me so much. No matter what they were, they fell simply, with a childlike candor from her.

"Well, their devotion was the main thing. Inseparable to an unbelievable degree. Far from the ordinary bond. They were each other's complement . . . if that explains it. . . . To make the story short, death spared one and took the other. For the survivor, life was unbearable, 'he living, Castor dead.' "

I stopped to blink my eyes that had been fastened so tightly on their heads that their presence had grown dim. Now I saw them clearly while she waited without interruption, without turning; she must have known I would continue.

"The story is that Pollux begged to share his own life with his dead brother. Each could live on alternate days—one would range the earth while the other remained below among the shades. One life divided between the two."

Her face lit up with comprehension. "So they were placed there side by side across the sky . . . always together . . . symbols of devotion . . . Gemini, the twins. I see them very clearly." She drew her eyes away till they were fully on me. Back in them lay that self-effacing look, that puzzled Signora Frola gaze of early evening, not yet destroyed. But through it something else of her looked out and met in calmness the eyes that studied her. Neither wavered in returning that searching inner gaze. I saw she shivered and took her arm.

"You're cold and never said a word. You'll have to interrupt me sometimes or I go on and on."

"But then, I might never know the choicest things." She lowered her head so that I barely heard her words. The spare illumination softened her face, obliterating its strong structure. I turned from time to time to watch how shadows became her.

There was a small outside light shining at the door of her house, so that the number 12 was heralded abroad out of all proportion to its size. We said very little else. It was somehow understood that we would see each other again. I touched her hand very briefly. She smiled, disengaging it with speed and grace to disappear behind the heavy door. I watched the house when she had gone, and saw its façade and its illuminated 12 disappear into the identical row of black shapes that faced the street. But for just a moment a tiny speck of light remained, an afterglow, like a piece of star that dove again into the dark sky.

(4)

IN THE months that followed, how many times I searched that lovely face for its particular look, its abiding expression, this or that quality that was peculiar to it! Was there something like a center to which the eye was drawn, and which somehow summed up an individual appearance, lent to it an original cast, marking off forever each single face from all its fellows? While it appeared there must be just such an individualizing trait, it was a maddening task to search it out in people you felt close to.

It confounded me in Laura, for she seemed to be so thoroughly unique; no one else looked remotely to my mind as she looked. But to what could I attribute this singularity of appearance? True, there was that unusually luminous texture of the skin, so striking

on first meeting, but neither its whiteness nor soft-
ness was its secret charm, but rather, the very absence
of color that compelled awareness. When she was
very young, she once explained, over a period of
time, she lost all pigment of the skin. She saw it, before her eyes, dissolve, fall away; and from the
splotchiness that intervened had finally come this
alabaster film so striking to the eye, this fragile illusion of white, the more attractive because it was not
real. But her coloring was not the "center" of her
being, not what made it singular. It was, first of all,
deception, elusive and illusory at once; and then
again, it was dispersed, when what I sought was
just the opposite, a focal point, the mysterious, re-
ducible component that accounted for her particular
face. There were the eyes, of course, but even they
shared her obliqueness. I could barely make out their
composition for the messages that obscured their
shape and color. Sometimes Signora Frola might be
fastened on the glance—a suffering, protesting look
—and I would be so rapt in that that nothing of the
eye itself was seen for this intrusion. Yet as weeks
passed, Signora Frola grew fainter there, and I finally
discerned more clearly flecks of color in themselves,
that complex maze of tints that we call hazel eyes—
greens, browns, blues, and grays each vying for su-
premacy that passed from one to the other, appearing and receding without reason, predominating for
as little cause as weather, the change of scene, unusual hues of dress. Even in this, I was left without
that "center" of appearance that I sought, for the
fluctuating tints of her eyes were no more definite,
graspable, than their covered messages or the non-

color of her skin.

If the uniqueness was not lodged in some isolated factor—the idea of a characteristic center was, after all, only postulation—was there something about the whole of personal appearance, the total accumulated effect, that set people off from one another, even to as unexacting an instrument as the naked eye, which would rather seek out duplication and similarity if given any choice, if left to its own devices of selection? There was something singular in the particular combination of features that produced Laura—but what? Or, to put it still another way, what was it in her that produced in *me* that slight start of surprise, a small inevitable lifting of my body, when I saw her or intercepted her glance? I could get that far in my speculation but no further, for if I resurrected her image in my mind, there was only a vague shape with a peculiar whiteness and a slight flickering of the eyes that stood for her. Only that much, but I recognized it as Laura without question, from my response to the smallest clue my memory had fastened upon to reproduce her presence. The attentiveness of my whole nervous system, revitalized and quickened, testified to its success, which, while it could not transmit the details of her being, had recreated the sense of it. Without my being able to locate or define it when I was with her, that something that distinguished her from everyone else had communicated itself to me. I had even imbibed it, so that in my thoughts and dreams she could be faceless, almost a specter, but still I knew her. While it struck me as peculiar that she could have so indefinite a form, I remembered that I, too, was faceless in my dreams, more faceless than she, and yet I knew who it was that passed in such endless parade through the high adventure and strange torpor of the night. Perhaps, then, she was closer to me than I thought, already close enough to erase the layers of detail that mark off the stranger who is seen more clearly against a wall of isolation. Yes, one could more easily perceive the outside. . . .

Those were the thoughts I thought when I was all alone, musing about her, or when in her company but not part of what she did and so could watch her from a distance. One such day I studied her appearance with more freedom than I generally allowed myself when she was watchful. I sat on the doorstep, a spectator, while she stood several yards away on the snow-covered lawn of the house in which she lived. A snowman was slowly rising from the level ground, an expanding hump, patted and smoothed, now by her, now by the landlord's small daughter waiting to see what Laura did, duplicating each motion seconds after her, making it seem an unsynchronized pantomime that unfolded on the snow-white stage before my eyes.

In the snow they looked of a piece just then, both small in a little-girl way—both bundled in snowsuits of navy blue, furry caps covering their heads, mittens obscuring any sense of fingers, heavy boots making them clumsy in the wide field of white. They looked like two dressed-up bear cubs, the way they grappled in the snow, clumsily stamping it from their feet—two frolicking bear cubs who bent and straightened in their play to imitate the human child. I had to laugh at them, particularly at Laura, who

took the making of a snowman with such seriousness. There she stood, away from it, biting her lip,
turning to examine it again, patting the sides softly,
pressing on more snow. Even in her gestures, she
seemed no more than a child then. I could imagine
her the size of the landlord's girl, with just that intent expression on her face, finishing a task, getting
it right. It still came out in her; I had noticed it before. To me it was an endearing, fleeting glimpse at
that small residue of childhood, half conjecture, that
faded as suddenly as it had appeared. But thought
of her possible past fascinated me; the idea that she
might have looked as she looked then, reduced in
size and fuller of face, and at another time in other
circumstances might have had this same expression,
something quite different causing her to squint or
throw that pensive smile behind her at another small
companion who followed at her heels, stirred my
curiosity. What had she been as a child beyond that
short glimpse suggested by attire and a momentary
childish absorption? What imaginings had overtaken her in those early years to produce with the passage of time the young girl that she became? Where
had those schoolgirl's thoughts disappeared, or what
had brought them back to earth again to mature to
the half-woman she was today? Much as I would
have liked it, there was no prodding other pictures
from my storehouse of memories, for only recently
had it acquired any of Laura at all, and those strictly
present-day, since I had access to no others. There
was only this accidental meeting with her childish
look and gesture, only that much might I know of
her past. The rest was shrouded by the white silence

of her face, that, for me, could stand only for the present moment. It was all that I might have if I were vouchsafed to have it at all. Since it was less than I coveted but perhaps more than I deserved, I continued to look at that embodiment of the very present that had produced the intertwining of our two, separate lives, unfortunately bereft of a common past.

Laura put finishing touches on the snow face, working over it as though it were the raw bone that the sculptor fashioned into flesh and the appearance of life. She stepped back to look at it, smiling a little, her exact movement and distance imitated by the child, who then could not contain her pleasure and flung herself on Laura, twining small arms about the other's legs, rooting her to the snow. A brush of white palm marks stood out sharply on the dark snowpants, marking the place where Laura had been caught in that quick motion of possession, so short-lived, for she was already advancing toward me while the girl abandoned the snowman and ran off to call her friends.

"Look at that," Laura said, pouting a little, "it's snowing again. In an hour he'll be blurred and covered, as though we hadn't made him at all."

"He wasn't made to survive." I laughed. "But let's put it to some constructive use . . . a walk, perhaps."

"Doesn't it seem strange? The very first winter we've seen together." She folded her arm over mine and dropped her head, pensive, as the flakes fell over us.

I watched the snow dot her hair, great white beads twined in soft black that waved out of sight under her furry cap. It melted into her face, white on white, leaving a cool dampness there, even trickling down her cheeks.

"Wait a minute," I said, "let me wipe you off a bit." I brushed the film of water from her face with my handkerchief, stopping to touch a place on her cheek with my finger, wanting to hold on to the spot, press it tightly, as that adoring child had folded herself about the bundled legs.

There was nothing of the child about Laura now. In her face and glance, the slight sway of her walk, was a self-possession and womanliness that could not be known in the oblivious child or in the overly conscious striving of the young girl. In her eyes there was no Signora Frola. More brown stood out in them, but I saw that they still were unclear. Something stood in the way of looking deeply into them, as Signora Frola used to do, but this was a different film imposed on the shifting color. We had resumed our walk.

"I wonder how it is that people begin to act. It must start very young." I still hoped to arouse some vision of her childhood.

"Oh yes—a long time ago for me." She might have preferred to let it go at that, but still, she found it hard to be evasive and had not the lightness to fashion a quick, facetious remark. With her, a casual question bore inward and assumed a greater weight from her intentness.

"It's not the same as 'just pretending.' The things you read must be the realest things of all. . . ." She smiled, remembering what it had brought to mind. "Like Cleopatra. . . . It's such a lovely sound. I think when I first heard the name, it was the ring of it I loved. And then, almost at once, I had to fill it up, give it a shape—a voice and body—place her on her special throne, make pyramids take shape, and river barges glide toward shore. How was it possible she wasn't living? . . . The vision was so clear. She came alive, slim and beautiful, painted with those striking colors made of clay. I could stretch myself before the mirror, put a headpiece on my hair, a cloak about my shoulders, and feel that, far from a dead thing, she was welling up inside me, taking shape there in the glass, and the Laura who watched moved farther back of her, until she was barely there at all. *I* was invisible and *she* was there." She stopped, transported to the present and to me, still not ready to be matter-of-fact, but less enraptured than before. "Acting is really that—a re-creation, like bringing someone back to life." She gave a short laugh. "Why, think of it, I raise Lazarus twice a year—only it's Juliet, Ophelia, Lady Macbeth. I breathe life into their nostrils as any God might do, and then I must *be* that Lazarus, too."

Now she became unexpectedly, untypically gay from her high excitement.

"Take a good look at me, then close your eyes. Oh, please do! because . . . I'm going . . . very slowly . . . to disappear."

When she finally whispered that I might look, I found her standing peculiarly still, clutching in her hand the broken end of an icicle, her hair freed from the furry cap, falling loose and disheveled about the neck.

"Am I to guess?" She did look, for the moment, with wide, staring eyes, startlingly different.

"My taper." She laughed and thrust forward the stick of ice. "Well—" she saw I had not understood —"it's just an introduction. By curtain time, I'll be much more convincing. It's my new part—Lady Macbeth." She said the name grandly, as though it were a magic sound, already filling.

She shivered, partly from excitement, a little from cold. The snow was falling faster now and became tangled in our lashes, catching on our lips, tasting cold and saltless on the tongue.

"It's blinding and delicious." Laura held her face out to it happily before we ducked for cover.

"Yes," and I leaned down to kiss her cheek as lightly as any snowflake had done.

(5)

I'M NOT, as a matter of fact, opposed to dignity. It's the only thing that makes some people bearable. If they did not hold themselves back, as a matter of form, who knows what indignities would be perpetrated in the name of their abandon. So, by all means, let them be as dignified as they like—let them fold their hands in church when the pastor describes *their* adultery, let them tip their hat to the client they have conned in their dignified way, let them pronounce the insidiously unfounded rumor they can install with careful restraint into a conversation. Let them have their dignity, but, in the end, let them be quiet, let them stand aside or remove themselves in the presence of the natural and greater dignity of death.

When Dr. Wengel died, it was not unexpected. A man over seventy years old has already died many times in his own fantasy and in that of people who watch him shuffle back and forth once a week with his piteous old man's walk. All that remained was the manner of his death, and that we had no occasion to see. But no one was surprised when he failed to appear one day, and no one had to look too closely at the carefully typed card tacked on the door: Class canceled—Death of Dr. Wengel. The presence of the teacher, which had made us a class, had been withdrawn, and there no longer being one, all who read the notice hurried away, strangely singular at a time when only collective demands had been made on them before, their individuality reviving in them with discomfort at eleven o'clock on Tuesday.

Dr. Wengel's family, with a different sense of his dignity than he might have had, whisked him from sight almost the same day in a private ceremony that some said ended in cremation, though that hardly seemed consistent with his views. It was a great misfortune that he did not lie in state, for few men could have received the court of that long, wordless reception line with the awe and dignity his silence would have lent to the occasion.

But, in fact, several days passed before official notice was taken of the death of the most celebrated teacher the university had ever produced. Again it took the form of a printed notice to the effect that a memorial service would be held at the hour of the class, and it was expected that the entire student body would attend. The date and time appeared slightly larger, in different type from the other words, giving the curious effect of dissociation from what the notice said. It was apparent from the way the days passed without formal attention to his death except on white printed cards that the administration believed itself to be handling this "situation" in the most dignified manner possible.

At the appointed time the student body gathered in the Theater Hall, the largest auditorium on the campus, where only grand events took place, and faced a row of shrouded figures behind an imposing lectern. Only when everyone was seated and the organ played the stately music that always heralds the academic march, were the shrouds restored to their ordinary guise, worn at all official functions, having nothing to do with the particular occasion that inspired their reappearance at this time. The procession moved forward, as though invoked by the opening chord and summoned unalterably to place —scholars in long, black robes—their academic standing in garish relief about their necks and shoulders, not even suppressed for an occasion usually marked by unyielding black—continuing their lugubrious entry down the aisles. Everyone stood, looking to see who passed, and remained standing for a quite ordinary invocation that might have inaugurated the opening day of school or the Christmas observance just as well, and which was read in the trained, oracular voice separating Sunday from every other day of the week.

Everyone sat down, and a waddling speaker with a handful of notes came forward. I had no sensation so great as that a degree was to be conferred that day. I almost scanned the stage for the honored guest, and remembered with a grotesque wince that Dr. Wengel could not possibly be present. Phil and I stared at each other in disbelief as one platitudinous speaker succeeded another eulogizing his "departed colleague," his "devoted friend as well as great scholar." Only with a vague sense of why we had come did we know these phrases to stand for Dr. Wengel, now bereft even of a name. Phil gave a half-audible moan that reminded us both of that long-ago day in class when he had jumped to his feet in interruption, with Dr. Wengel at his desk looking over our heads, intoning Phil's name in his resonant voice, "Yes, Mr. Richter, yes." It was the only moment in all the circumlocutions regarding him, his death, in which he seemed to appear either dead or alive, or even to *have been* in any real sense.

Phil craned his neck at something in sudden agitation, rising, muttering excuses as he left his seat. People around us seemed ruffled by his inappropriate exit, but I could see by their concern that some of them overcame their indignation with the thought that he might have been taken ill. I remained in my seat and glanced wearily at the new speaker, who was using almost the same words as the first eulogist except that this voice was weaker, less commanding, and conjured more coughs in its wake on that account.

The drone of his words was cut off in mid-consonant with thunderous violence, like the unexpected roar of an earthquake, shocking everyone alert. The appalling resonance of the organ swelled through the architecture, its fused sounds suspended in a tremulous chord, separating at last, breaking apart to proclaim *The Art of Fugue* to ears familiar with its complex interwinding sounds. It was the most vigorous, aggressive affirmation of life possible in that deadened atmosphere, and it rolled on sonorously, with its grand gesture and protest, to the final chilling chord dying away with a faint echo into the finally frozen silence. A far different hush had spread through the hall, and the long, unrelieved, expired sound was the tensest realization of Dr. Wengel's death that could have been expressed. Eyes were cast down or glued on the patch of organ loft dwarfed by the dimensions of the grand auditorium. I knew it was Phil who rose against the backdrop of enormous brown pipes before he turned to rush down the stairs and out of the building.

With his flight, the service was suddenly ended, the speaker still at his place on the stage and the students pressing against each other pell-mell into the aisle ahead of the shocked scholars, not yet formed for the recessional. Yet there seemed to be more dignity in those confused moments when dignity had been scattered than there had been in all the proprieties of the more formal observance. I retreated in the midst of a circle of outraged faculty members in their black robes, beside themselves with agitation that spread through their ranks. From among them a restrained whisper circulated: "Look there—it's Stermer! . . . Stermer's here. . . . No respect, even for the dead." I saw where they pointed, without raising a hand, to the last row. Lost in its middle, isolated and alone, a man sat there, disheveled, his hair unsettled, his collar open at the neck, something about him torn, neglected—such disregard of personal appearance as is never seen in a public hall. He glanced at no one, seemed equally unaware of their interest and distaste, now walking past even the lone gowned figure who approached him, embarrassed, with extended hand, in behalf of all the rest. He left without attention to anything in that place, without a word, in his seedy suit, with the utmost dignity, making it abundantly clear that he, for one, had known Dr. Wengel had lived.

(6)

T H E world, so long solitary, had rapidly filled with people. In the midst of study, reading, or that general wide contemplation I indulged in as I walked, I would be overtaken by thoughts of one or another of them. Some recollection of Laura, Phil, or Connie might infiltrate what I was doing, or something they had said evolved into a provocative scene my fantasy would construct around them.

Then I thought I might even leave off reading for a while to savor more fully the rich drama of intimacy with others. It had the quality of involving one deeply, of drawing one in, at first unawares, and steeping one more and more in the specialized world in which small groups insulate themselves. So totally did it absorb one into the delimits of its particular time and place, that it rivaled the beckoning arm of history that by an arbitrary motion obscured a wider view, lifting moments out of the scale of the past into the foreground of the mind. The effect was even more immediately compelling than that long arm of history clutching the collar, leading one from the mount of Xenophon along the precipice of the known world, through the glutted, serpentine streets of cacophonous Alexandrian bazaars, to a Rome deserted of citizenry, resounding with incredulous cries of pillagers, shattering prizes for clumsy joy. For the moment, it drove one deeper into hidden places of the mind, closer at hand, more open to examination than the petulant envy of Plato, the cool hauteur of Aristotle, the excessive candor of St. Augustine. This intimate circle of live beings, still becoming, installed into my life an exhaustive, omnivorous interest in the incredible everyday lore that is man's relation to man.

Often we walked four abreast on the sidewalk, so deeply involved that we barely noticed the inconvenience we caused to the passage of others. Only when compelled by unequal numbers did we break apart for however long was necessary before recombining forces to resume our long, leisurely walks. Then we would have to fling exchanges, remarks, and interruptions across the girth of our little band from one end to another.

The attention that we stirred provoked great pride in me, for we must have been an imposing quartet walking past—oversized Phil on one end punctuating vigorous remarks with the gestures of his enormous hands; Connie by his side, majestic, titanesque, throwing her head back to laugh her womanly laugh, all the while tucking loose strands into the heaped, honey-colored mound on her head; Laura, average-size by other standards, looking diminutive beside the other two, until something in the intensity of the soft, sharp outline of her face leaped out to offset disparity of size; and, too, she was restored to normal stature by the average size of the companion walking with a touch of proprietary exaltation by her side. . . .

Laura drew attention on other counts as well. Many who stopped to talk became intrigued by that unnatural whiteness so baffling to the unaccustomed eye, leading it, on that account, to overattentive stares along the circumference of her face where the contrasting dark cloud of hair was brushed in irregular waves from the widow's peak to the shoulder, curving gently inward to touch the neck. Others who knew her regarded her always in some surprise, for those same compelling features could elevate her on one occasion to a brooding beauty and on another accentuate an overharshness of line, verging on the unattractive. This was because her features were often in an altered relation to one another—some of the time in harmony, none too dominant; yet other times the nose seemed thrust too starkly from the cavity of eyes, or else the eyes themselves were over-round and prominent, casting an illusion of daintiness over the lower face. She was like those women one would know how to admire on a stage, or in an opera box, perhaps, but not fully appreciate transposed to the level of the street where the gravity of their features could not adequately project themselves without distortion.

There was, too, the shy recognition of strangers in her local renown, though it went unremarked by her. Some who passed half smiled, as many do who know a face from some moment on the stage, expecting neither acknowledgment nor return of their unspoken greeting, only the simple pleasure of a small encounter. And when, on one or two occasions, she noted the pause and smile and paused herself, turning a questioning glance on the familiar look, the moment was destroyed, and with quickened, embarrassed step the admirer moved on, leaving Laura wondering almost naïvely who it was who had passed, or asking with incongruous modesty if something in her appearance were, perhaps, awry. . . .

Often Connie would wait until Phil was his most eloquent to interrupt his careful argument with her gift for mimicry. Then there might issue from her womanly throat the deep, portentous, stage-solemn voice of the theater director we all knew. It was thrust into the conversation with such consummate flair and dramatic timing that we could only roar with laughter and abandon all else in the face of this distraction. With a swift mobility of face and voice, a look, a gesture, she could catch in someone just the precise, peculiar traits engendering him. So, with only a half-turn toward us, taking her ear between the thumb and index finger of one hand, rubbing back and forth along the lobe as though handling the softest fabric, she could evoke the physical presence of someone remote, like Laura's landlady. But she was even more successful in mimicking the near-at-hand, like the mock seriousness of Phil, which—by tilting slightly back, the skeptic in her eye, hands and mind impatient in their motion, running in advance of speech—she could convey in the sparest gestures. With those quick, agile turns, she could suggest two poles which were his nature: an occasional professorial air and a suppressed hilarity, the mockery in him that underlay the scholar. At such times, Phil laughed loudest of all, enjoying the raillery for itself, not caring that it was at his expense. It was also through Connie's sly thrusts that I first noted a mannerism of Laura's that had not seemed remarkable before—the way the fingers of one hand lay cupped along the eyebrow when she thought or listened, a little like the famous gesture of Rodin's *Thinker,* displaced to the upper face by several inches.

Most memorable of all perhaps, at least to me, was the day she waved us silent to launch another imitation. She began to speak with a ponderous dignity of speech, very deliberate, with long pauses between phrases and a trailing off of voice to find the properly weighty word, a felicitous turn of phrase. Still dissatisfied, she stopped to start again. This time she took a small idea which she overelaborated with explanation until it had become mortifyingly complex. But she broke off again, still in some frustration, to project still a third impression, remaining silent for this attempt, and leaning far forward, her face strained with earnestness, as though trying to communicate were some extraordinary effort. Then she fell back at last, as though listening to an invisible speaker, but even then, with an eagerness to participate, she began nodding vigorously as the supposed "other" spoke, as some people do to music— a "My sentiments exactly" or "A good point" that escaped silently in that repeated and vigorous nod. Laura had lowered her head to smile and Phil laughed outright.

With a tardy wince of illumination, I caught the extra touch of rascality in Connie's face, and finally recognized something of myself held up to friendly ridicule. In momentary confusion, I wondered if the naked, outside eye were any truer than our blind insulation. I laughed with them uneasily, warily, as one does at those grotesque images, barreled and squat or waveringly thin that gaze back at us in that room of distorted mirrors at the Carnival Hall. . . .

Forming, as we did, a little band, we drew people around us who were often alone, and from time to time our foursome was augmented by those who longed, themselves, to be part of just such a group. In the coffee shop, where we were well known, we invariably held the favored spot by the window, where we could look across the campus and gaze at the season's change in trees and the year's permanence in concrete, and where, too, we could be spied in the low frame of the window by people we knew who drifted in to join us. The most interesting ones were always off after a fast exchange, for they were always engaged in their own work and their own affairs and returned straightaway to them. Others stayed interminably, like Dick Goff, who was so nearsighted he had almost to peer into a face to recognize it. His glasses were so thick that a smokiness formed the inside rim, and the contracted iris blinked as he talked. His nearsightedness should have been a distinct liability, for he was a professional circulator of petitions, and it was only sheer determination and willfulness that led him unerringly to his prey. He had a pencil ready behind one ear, a pen clipped to his shirt, and the folded end of his current petition flapped in his back pocket. It could be of any conceivable kind—antivivisectionist, in support of organic foods, for compulsory birth control in slum areas, for reconsideration of Indian rights as citizens, or for social-security benefits for artists. He cleared a space in front of him, wiping the table clean with a napkin, unfolding his papers with elaborate pomp before launching into his vigorous invective of the day, for though his petition was usually *for* something, its sponsor argued the negative case. As Connie once said, she hadn't the heart to tell him she would sign anyway. Thus, when he squinted in at the window, we resigned ourselves to our fate, Phil enlivening it with controversy and Laura restive with questions. If he left with our signatures, he felt it a signal victory.

We greeted Arnold Hendries, who waved at us from the door, in an altogether different way. He was a serious person and good company, except for occasional silent lapses. He knew Laura from the very first day he had entered the university. They had struck up a conversation in an office vestibule while waiting for scholarship forms, and companionless and lonely, he gratefully looked upon her as an old friend. Whenever he appeared, his violin preceded him as he moved between tables, for he came for coffee as a release after long hours in the practice rooms. As he neared us, he moved forward an extra chair on which with great solicitude to lay his instrument. One wondered on seeing him that he was a violinist, for his posture seemed stooped, given to drooping, and he was easily depressed. But Laura, having heard him play, assured us he was different in recital, erect, poised, suggesting boldness more than anything, and enormously gifted. He sensed her admiration and would hurry over, relieved to find us there, eager to talk. I noticed after a while that whatever the subject, he introduced sums into the conversation—the press of money was his bane—the price of tickets, the cost of this article or that, the rumor of new fees, the saving, the increase, the ceiling in rent. He had moved three times already. Low on funds, he was harried by neighbors who complained of his long hours of practice and landlords who perpetually banged at his door. We rejoiced with him when at last he found just the place, a loft above a printing shop. During the day he could never stay there, for the din of the presses precluded any morning or afternoon habitation. But at night, when the whole business district closed down and that part of the city ceased to exist for all but him, he could play to his heart's content as late as he pleased. Even in the listening, one felt a comradely joy at the thought of those unending cadenzas pouring into the drab, mercantile streets.

He ran over to us in great excitement one day, bobbing up and down as he talked. He had been signed for a summer tour; he would play all over Central America, going even as far as Colombia and Ecuador. Plans overflowed from him—his first tour, the prospects it opened, the money he had been advanced, the things he would need: a supply of strings, his own suit—not borrowed or rented this time—his violin specially treated to withstand the tropics, fungi, and all that. And he busily calculated sums, dropping figures here, adding them there, patting the chair where the violin lay, in a delirium at this change of fortune.

When he left, Connie rolled her head distractedly, an incoherent stream of words rushing out in imitation, reducing the variety of his confused joy to this hopeless babble.

"My God, he's better off depressed. This way—" and she repeated the effusion a second time, with a sly grin, ending it with an effeminate gesture of the hand. We halfheartedly responded to her jest, though Laura was visibly annoyed. Connie, for her part, was dismayed and crestfallen that her observation was obviously no new discovery to any of us. Phil commented that he had seen it in Arnold at once, but, after all, it had nothing to do with us. Laura remarked that there was a certain depth to him nonetheless, and people should be taken as they were. I would go further than any of them, I said. It seemed slighting to reduce people to such simple terms, to extract one element of a many-sided individual and assign a prescribed stamp to the whole. Connie was deflated at not being thought at the top of her humor; her jest had fallen a little flat. But more than that, she seemed stunned that we, all of us, should have had silent knowledge of something only apparent to her in a moment when it had burst out of control. Our perception and equanimity puzzled her. I remember she did not regain her spirits as we talked. It was the first time I had known her to brood.

Days later, when Arnold stood in the doorway making his way over to us, violin in hand, not pressing forward a chair this time, I saw that Connie winced, riveting her curious gaze on the rest of us who heard but restrained comment on his agitated fluctuating voice, and watched without censure his quickened womanly airs. Arnold, unaware, began almost at once. The tour was still on, he said, anxious to restore confidence—no, it wasn't that. It was his instrument. He had played hundreds of violins before settling finally on this one. It had exactly the right tone. He played it once, and it felt better under his chin, along his arm, in his ear, than any he had tried. It fit him exactly. Could we ever understand what that had meant? After waiting so long, to have found just the right one, depositing all his savings on it, falling into debt to own it. One violin in the world waiting somewhere for each violinist, and incredibly, at so young an age, he had found his.

"But they have taken away the tone." He seemed to tremble. "It can withstand everything now . . . heat, the dampness, the fungi . . . yes, at exactly the cost I told you. But—" he drew his breath with difficulty—"it has a thin voice now, not mine . . . the one I discovered when I raised my bow to it the first time." I thought of the thin voice now issuing from his larynx, so much more richly amplified through the sounding box of dark varnished wood. He could not continue, and forgetting the instrument lay on his lap, he rushed to retrieve it before it fell.

"But surely it's only temporary. How could they

do it all the time if the risk were so great?" Laura
looked at him with great, intent eyes, and a small
hope appeared at the words.

"They said, in a few months. . . . But suppose not
. . . that strange sound in my ear . . . the tour.
. . ." He broke off, and resumed almost philosophically. "You are luckier than we. . . . You, actors,
singers, dancers—you are your own instrument. Not
like us, dependent on a manufactured object, beautiful as it might be, but still a piece outside ourselves.
Something not integrally bound to us, physically—
not to our brain and being. Yes, you are luckier
than we."

"We are our own instrument," Laura repeated
the words curiously. "What a chilling thought. Wonderful but fearful, too. . . . A cracked voice is so
much more terrible than a sour note. But when it
issues full, just right, the mechanism itself is our
own, is *us*. Our own instrument. . . . But then, it
must be all inwardness, as fragile as we are, and so
much the harder if we fail. . . ."

Arnold only half heard her, was already moving
away, his shoulders stooped, his old air of depression
back, and we fell, at his departure, into a reflective
silence. The only movement for minutes was the
circling of Connie's eyes from one to the other of
us, questioningly, as though searching out the difference that marked us. Her restive glance hesitated at
Phil and remained rooted there, oblivious to the
other presences so recently passed over.

"What can you think about that it becomes so
quiet?" she asked at last.

"Just thoughts," Phil answered, still bemused and
pensive.

"There must be many thoughts I have no way of knowing—your thoughts, I mean. —You don't share them so easily."

Phil returned her gaze calmly. "Sometimes thoughts are only just being formed. When you share them, they already exist somehow. Not all thoughts are that kind."

"Oh, but there's a kind that comes from two people talking, a joint creation you might say, growing as they exchange ideas."

"Yes, there's that kind, too."

"No, not 'too'! It's more important than that." She leaned forward as she spoke. "I know I want to tell you everything I think, and I do, *I do*. —But, with you, there is such a small part of your mind that you surrender at once, so much that you never divulge at all. —I sometimes feel I'm part of that *everything* that interests you, not the final repository that is the one person you love."

"But I had no idea that love is . . . that. And yet, I think I feel it very deeply—in my way." He reached over the table for her hand and held it enclosed a moment in his. Laura and I exchanged uneasy glances. It seemed we should not be there; yet we were loath to stir lest we break the deepnesses and scatter them with our rising.

"Oh, you are a satisfactory lover—when you love." She smiled their secrets into the air but disentangled her fingers tentatively from his grasp. "Only, when people love, it is paramount to everything. The world falls into place around them; they are its natural center. *They, they* . . ."

"Yet one has oneself besides, even though the 'they' burns to the very heart . . . thoughts apart, a curiosity for the world. No betrayal."

"I'd be content if there were only you and I . . . no one besides, a world unto ourselves." I almost made as if to leave, but Laura sat transfixed, and I, too, felt a dizzy soaring, as though carried on rising wings of song, Isolde-ward, not meant to rest until the ascent had been made, unalterably complete. "All thoughts become one thought because they rest in us —the oneness that we are. —Oh, I know a love, what a love it is! But you must sink into it with the wholeness of your being, the wholeness that two people are. . . . Then it lifts you up, up . . . and it becomes what life is . . . and what life becomes without it."

Phil reached again for her hand, making it still, for her words rolled like the waves, circled like the clouds.

"My love is a different love," he said softly.

"You never tried mine! It might even be passing between us now in the thought you left unsaid. If you make it ours, you will see. Try *mine!*"

"But my thought was of the world, of Arnold and his violin, Laura and her instrument, of myself and the silence."

Connie drew in her breath while he spoke, filling her lungs with it. "No matter. It isn't silent any more. It is enough to join."

Their hands lay one in the other tightly; there was a moment's repose. My chair scraped as I rose; Laura's spoon fell as she stirred. We left them looking raptly at each other in the picture-frame window, where unseen crowds, we among them, passed by.

I gripped Laura's hand the harder as we walked, as though we, too, might consummate an act of love in the pressing together of our hands. They fell into place, mine atop hers, rubbing there, secreting juices, one into the other, but the motion of our walk kept them from becoming altogether still.

I was aware of an overwhelming tenderness for Laura, but I was hard put to know what it was. It was a tenderness I felt for women, the soft, dark things they were, but only Laura touched that place. I realized she urged up in me hidden things, mysterious, delicious, fearful thoughts that seemed connected with my whole life—that I could never have but for her. She tied me to past memories that gave me anchor and extended me beyond myself, so that the future seemed foreseeable, graspable, almost at hand, and I more omnipotent than I had ever dreamed of being. This tenderness came over me when I thought of this that she gave me without the guile to know it —something never withheld, never rationed, not demanded—a constant stirring-me-up but letting-me-be, a rare thing, and I was grateful.

That very moment, hands still linked, from walking nowhere in particular we were headed somewhere. We left for the nearby seashore, though it was already midafternoon, though it meant abandoning former plans, though it was still a chilly spring, for no reason but that I asked it. I knew where we must go. It was a place I had been to as a child, but I had stood on the edge of it, looking up from the flat beach to the high dunes where it stood, settled in between the ridges of sand and the strange seaside weed that grew there.

It was called the Pavilion and was an abandoned lookout from the heights to the beach and ocean, a shelter from wind and other elements in a place that the sea never reached. Once when I had approached the dunes, going farther than I had ever been, I saw two shapes huddled together on its weathered bench, and I looked wonderingly at this seat of highest mystery, leaving behind my solitary tracks, impressing a circular route in the sand, mute testimony to what I had fleetingly seen.

Now I returned there full-grown, finding the sea as poignant as I had then, and the beaches, empty of bathers and untidied by Nature, a desolate place. The waves, already frothy from the secret underwater contention that made them, were churned up by the wind. Laura walked in the sand beside me, holding her shoes in one hand, and with the other flattening the hair whipped in all directions by sea gusts. She seemed more abandoned than I had ever seen her, stirred up by the wind, unquiet. The onslaught was so great that we retreated farther from the water's edge, where she kept her head turned from the ocean, fully facing me and laughing at how we were buffeted along the beach.

"Strange . . . we think we know the beach, and then see it like this, wild and deserted. . . . I'm glad we came on an impulse . . . like this."

She stopped to slip into her shoes again, steadying herself against my arm while I looked out over the dunes for the Pavilion. The whiteness of the sand, softer there than where we stood, and the dry weeds swaying, set in motion tides of reverie. I looked across the dunes, fearful lest it might not be there. But with relief I saw it had survived the vagaries of weather and the succession of years. There it was! We approached, and my heart contracted at the sight of its dull gray-brown where I had remembered it white; it seemed stunted and small where I had thought it twice the size, commanding the heights. No matter, I said to myself, though disappointed that Laura should see *this* Pavilion and not the more impressive one I carried so faithfully through the years. But she made no sign that it was other than I had said, and once inside, the wide breadth of ocean visible from that high ground did not fail me. We were a piece of its beach, yet apart. Looking out at the ocean from afar, we were amazed how calm the sea seemed with its tiers of waves, indistinguishable but for their graceful white tips. Were it not for the rustle of weeds and the occasional lifting of sand before us, we would not have known the wind raged as it did by the shore. . . . The strange contradiction of appearances, dependent more than we think on the vantage point of observation . . . a second's thought then. . . . I remember it well.

We sat on the bench where we could touch the splintered railing with our bare feet and huddle close together, glancing from the sea to one another. Our bodies gradually pressed downward with the weight of love that made us sink to level ground, seeking the ultimate warmth of purely internal worlds. I wondered if wide, curious eyes watched us from some hidden corner of the dunes and thought us more important than we were. But with that passing thought, I left onlookers far behind, any who might have existed that wind-swept day, the small boy who paused nearby so many years ago, his footprints swept away as the sand was swept across the beach and under the sea, all the onlookers I had been my life long. There was only the pull of the undertow drawing me into the gray-blue sea of Laura's ocean-flecked eyes, pressing me toward the dark undersea places from which I came, deep under the cool surface, until reaching them, I felt like the centuries-old surge of ocean rising from dark caverns to meet the soft beach, with a great rush of power fixing the crest and slowly subsiding, almost imperceptibly sliding back into the oblivion of the sea again.

When, raising my head from the side of her neck, I saw Laura fully, again Laura, and what had joined us those moments ago over and aside, I felt baffled that she was there. In the high swirl of the sea, the undertow has already ceased to exist, and we, too, disappear to become the inundation. Mindful now of her, I could barely remember her participation. Rather, on recollection, I could only reconstruct an ease of disintegration, a welcomed obliteration, and that falling away of layer upon layer of her, pleasurably, until no modicum was left. Like the submergence, the temporary annihilation of herself into those roles of the stage, she had fallen away here, too, with a joyousness of abnegation. But she was returning, even under my gaze, still resisting, back into the folds of herself, and I thought, seeing the cool struggle, how distant her glance seemed from any thought of me, how unwarm her smile compared to that peak of intimacy. Watching her and viewing the ocean again, I felt one as inscrutable as the other, but my wonder nonetheless grew, deepened, as I quietly gazed at them again.

We walked by the shore again, the wind knocking

us together, we mindful of and grateful for the collision. The waves seemed menacingly high, and the Pavilion, as we looked back in the distance, looked like just another sand dune, a little higher than the rest.

"Look . . . already disappearing. Soon only a speck. Unseen by us, it can return to its peace again." Laura whispered it in my ear, sharing my frequent backward glance. As she spoke, she lifted the damp hair falling at her temple, moving it from her face, over and back, in an impatient, fretful motion.

Not sure why, I grasped her hand to arrest it in that act, coming to a stop on the sand.

"What is it?" she asked, hand already by her side.

The gesture was past. A wave had just left the beach, strewing bits and pieces of sea, eagerly rushing back headlong into water to become ocean again. —A brown hand that brushed temple, pushed back hair, a peevish thrust—that grandmother, so long a loved face framed in a thin, black border, for a moment nimbly plucking strands from her forehead . . . hands moving in rapid strokes, kneading, crocheting. Out there was the sound of the sea. She sat on the sofa, whose bristles she never noticed, with a thoughtful, absent air, off in thoughts of another sea, blue and faraway, not seeing that small eyes watched even that gesture through hair, every act important . . . hers. Wave knocked on wave, making one giant crest. She looked up swiftly, suddenly knowing eyes gazed even on absent thought. She smiled and curved the same fingers that lifted hair—to beckon me. The wave washed on the shore, a soft ripple of water. I sat on the highest seat in the world, the warm curve

of lap that took me up, clearing off for me my place
in the world, my shelter. The ocean reclaimed the
wave.

Laura's hands were languid, white as only those
without color are white . . . not heavy-veined, not
old . . . they loving, too . . . I, not made to watch
forever, circular footprints in sand. A new wave
formed, my own, full of the love that moved up in
me for that Laura who with a familiar thrust of the
hand joined old love and new, recovered lostnesses
grown too dim to see. She moored again a life set
afloat, adrift, not knowing it wandered. I took the
hand she gave into mine, and in its soft folds, its
warmth, its life, I clasped in a single moment what
once was and what had come to be, brought together
for the first time as though they were of one and the
same life.

We walked from the ocean, not able to leave it.
We stood watching it from still another place—on
the small length of boards at a thin, black rail—a
fourth time different . . . a sweeping gray, wider
still, the widest it had ever been, as though it existed
before beach, before us, before everything.

(7)

SOME places are so well known, impressions of
them overlap and become no longer single, vivid
ones, but composite, blurred shapes. It is impossible
to extract definite recollections of them, for they elude

association with any particular things—there is no particular incident, no particular person to make them precise, special memories.

There is that lovely Museum garden verging on the water, where people sit and talk, and when silent watch the mosses and water lilies swim apart and pigeons scurry along the precipice. But it is the same for everyone who goes there; that is what it is and that is all that happens at any time. I went there only the other day at lunchtime, when it was full of people coming and going and less tranquil than in the leisurely late afternoon when one can sit immobile for hours over coffee, undisturbed by a single thought, carried along by the combined closeness of water and the proximity of all those people talking softly, enjoying the same gentle outdoors. I have been there too many times with too many people for it to elicit in retrospect more than these vague, general observations.

There is the airport where I have gone on so many hot nights, for it is far removed from the congested air of the city; a fresh breeze stirs there when there is stillness everywhere. And I have watched planes land and make numerous false starts, and watched people file decorously onto the runway and less decorously off it, and seen them gather in tense bunches at the gate. And when I have noted these impressions, I have said what all those nocturnal visits have been.

Or then again, I have looked at so many mammoth chandeliers in theaters, concert halls, reception rooms —the kind that are monumentally still or those that sway every so often from side to side or, the most fascinating of all, those that seem to tip over just a fraction and rivet our attention on that account. One would think that all those glistening crystals, better able to reflect than rough, unresponsive surfaces, could retain a truer image. But none of these places, worn over in the mind, can inspire a single, clearcut, unalterable memory. Out of all the impressions they have given, there is no preserving the substance of any of them.

But the place you have been to only once, that can bring to mind one time and one person only, and then again, something special about that once into the bargain—there you have something sharp to summon at the very sound of the name. "Ah yes—that small pavilion on the beach at Sea Heights." And there is only one it could be and only one time it existed, and it is only Laura who shared it. . . .

Just such a memory of place attaches to the City Aquarium, where Phil and I spent several hours once. I have not been back to see it since, and so it is one of those places that, when its name is pronounced, elicits the backdrop of a whole day and recalls the entire duration of our visit in its long, resonating halls and strangely silent rooms.

First, there was that first impression—crossing from the threshold into the room. The light was startling! Outside, the gloom of final winter days; within, the dull fluorescence of the hall; but through that doorway a clear, white light suffused the room. Aquarium lamps, hung over tanks, cast warmth and brightness on the swarms of life that swelled the quiet waters. Brightly illumined, they rose in bold relief against the lamps' persistent glow.

Then the colors that one saw there! Striped and speckled and solid-hued, colors leaped out without accompanying form in that first sweeping glance, where red and purple, orange and green alarmed the eye with sudden being and swift demise. The colors reappeared in still newer combination, the whole a work of art in progress before one's very eyes, the unfettered chaos the artist sees, congestions of ideas heaped on the mind until he burrows through and fixes permanently their form.

I turned to look at Phil, amazed. I saw by his smile of satisfaction that he had hoped for just this effect, the drab-sounding Aquarium becoming paradoxically quite opposite in reality, my dubious interest inflamed by the unexpected brilliance of this entry into the room.

Up close we could examine particular shapes and forms that from afar did not exist. The volatile specks that darted in and out were apprehended in their flight. One saw their sudden stirrings were in response to other life. Even lonely wanderings seemed something of a search. At sight of their own kind, the strays lunged forward to join little bands that formed, the lives of many strangers thus strung together in long lines of silent company, to which each member was attracted by glimpse of coral hues and bloated shapes that matched their own. In some secluded place, through filigree arms of plants, ringed bodies swam to amorous coves where twosomes dallied. Their movements coincided in their lingering, and there in the tangles of dark green they skirted one another, alternating their approaches and retreats with a long, gliding embrace that marked their courtship. In some, black rings were tapered at both ends, their middle girth much greater than the rest; in others, the bands were uniform to match proportions that were equally wide from tip to toe. In all encounters, of whatever kind, a near-immobility reigned in between the darting. Such languidness held sway that those same shapes that glided past remained suspended whole moments without moving. There was a tranquil side to their communal life —those semidormant states, the way they fed on willing plants that stretched their arms to aid the nibbler, the trail of baby fish, still imprecise of turn, colliding with another. Intent upon their everyday, we found in all first glimpses of that ocean life, a peace and gentleness, a world bland and benign that we who watched could only hope to emulate.

And then another layer of submarine existence would unfold. One would espy a deadly stalking among ferns. The calmness of a sheltered place was overlain with ripples where no friendly interlude took place, but by a flash of pink one saw the swift pursuit of some small shape. Or without warning, no chance to rush for cover or lose the enemy in slippery folds of plants, a silent swooping broke peace with neighboring life. Nothing recorded or remarked the snatching of that one lithe, silver form, so beautifully aquiver before a single, fearful inhalation banished it forever from the world. Others were luckier than that. Entwined in moss, mere wisps of fish stirred nervously within their refuge while hungry stalkers prowled nearby, full of Scalere boldness and assurance.

Some had no need of violent death. It swam in

them, was rising higher even as their svelte, black bodies pressed against the glass. Their playful brethren, some mixed with white, circled beside them. Together they leaped high into the air, restraining their high spirits in delight of falling, as though it were a game. Even as they frolicked, one saw the mark of early death in some. The telltale sign already showed beneath dissolving black in small green spots, by which, in contrast to its mystery in the wider world, death here made known intentions and its prey.

In exile, in lonely isolation from the rest, the brooding Bettas trailed graceful arms behind them, like great, dangling sleeves they pulled along the water's edge. So fierce their rages, they were made solitary to preserve the peace communal tanks required to survive. But enforced solitude had made these fighting fish more beautiful than before. Like artists maturing in lonely retreat, they turned subtle and bright, mixing the reds, the purple shades in startling combination to form hues unknown to any spectrum and beauty unprecedented in that world.

Along the bottom of each tank, another mode of life went on. The scavengers of that abundant life lay waiting between fronds for kindnesses that death deposited without the asking at their feet. Minuscule shellfish of every size and shape were scattered along the floor, and snails, especially, writhed their heads loose from lethargic sleep. Among them flora of every kind—white and ridged or smoothly blue, translucent puffy wisps or statuesque and stolid shapes—swayed along the water where clinging algae and mosses also formed. They made opaque films that sought to hide from view that remarkable variety and abundance that lived within those walls of glass.

By then Phil and I had gone full circle through the room. We stood again at that same doorway where we had entered, struck by that first sight of accentuated light, that formless color, the panoramic view of what we had so lately studied in great detail.

I thought to myself it was a miniature ocean, a small universe. My mind thought back to that time eons ago in dark waters where light was just filtering in, when none of this variety and movement yet existed. Somewhere in that darkness turning light and that frigidity becoming warm—life began. The thought was suddenly exciting. Who knew how or when, or what possible combustion of chemical and water caused it? Did we know even that it happened in quite that way—first none, then one, then many? If so, some saline fecundity became a living cell, capable of making itself over an indeterminate number of times, with virtuosic ability to become all of that variety that had left us almost breathless, millions of years after the fact, that first fact that engendered all of these possibilities.

"It staggers the imagination." I turned to Phil. "Imagine a principle that could encompass all this diversity and abundance!"

Phil refused to bend now to the naïve sense of wonder that had been unmistakably on his face when we had toured the room. We had been too absorbed with what we saw to notice each other, but once or twice I had seen his expression. His face had been pinched together in the closest scrutiny as he leaned over, his eyes level with whatever had taken his interest, widening with excitement at each new discovery. Full of a primitive enthusiasm not yet disguised, he had motioned me over with hectic gesturing to share those moments of particular fascination that so absorbed him. Now he put aside what he frequently would rather that no one saw, in order to become what he loved best, the man who stood above the mystery, turning naïve experience into the guise of more subtle speculation. With a brush of the hand he dismissed expression of those feelings I knew had been aroused in him.

"We have here only the possibilities that worked out. What of those others that failed? We are certainly no worse off for them. Yet the original hypothesis includes them, too." He held his cupped hand to one side of the nose and mouth as he considered it, glancing out into the air. "If one could live a life with as much invention, postulate even the most farfetched possibilities with the same adventure, and feel nothing is lost if some may fail!"

We still stood in the doorway and took a final look at the luminous panorama of life swarming in those enormous tanks. I turned from that abundant universe to regard Phil, the enigmatic figure beside me, a single specimen, not an abstract possibility but concretely present, one of the infinite possibilities with which I had credited that first life. As we turned this last time to review the flutter, the color, the shapes suspended about the room, I saw the curious admiration creep again into his eyes.

"Life on the smallest scale," he might have remarked if he had allowed himself the luxury. I smiled to see him swept up again in what we saw, almost against his will. He would have been happier to postulate, as he had said, programs of thought and action, all possible variation worked through beforehand, even reflection on failure considered by the way. But I saw he was, as much as any, impulsive and apt to contradict hypotheses that he embraced by some spontaneous act.

I remember him most clearly in that place. His blondness that rose above a few dark crests of hair— he was, too, brown of eyes, not even fair of skin, but seeming more blond for all of that—appeared more striking within that room of light. His head thrown back, he might have addressed the air; his hands, overlarge, all joints and knuckles, accompanied the words that followed crisply from his abstract thought. When he was wry, astringent—as he could be—there was suggested a smile repressed to add more humor. All those I see in that same Phil who stands framed in that doorway. The vision is so much what he was then, he seems embodied in that room, a chamber of the mind that holds him fast, and yet—so small a part was fixed there, so infinitesimal a piece of that moving, shifting figure remains true. They are alive— aquarium room and fish, conversation and Phil—and dead, too, embalmed in a false preservative simulating life where it has long since disappeared. After it has been extolled and honored, summoned and rebuffed, is that, in the end, what memory is, the rigidifying fluid on the mortician's shelf? Those bottled formulae had not fooled me as a child, nor do they now, when they beguile with life and are lifeless.

Yet, if they are to exist, those most important adjuncts of my life, my grandmother, Phil, Laura—and they *must* survive, for they are part of *me*—I am at the mercy of that great preserver, false though it may be, stopping where life only starts, ever still where the other ever moves. And yet, when I have said all that, I must be grateful to memory. It has a grandeur augmented with time, which with age becomes more precious than the ephemeral passage of days.

(8)

THERE is no restraining Phil. He has engaged the memory, not to relinquish its stage until he is ready to recede from view. Almost invisibly, he alters appearance and attire to accommodate a change of scene. Crossing from aquarium room to club, he exchanges a boyish smile for formal bearing and ordinary casual dress for the elegance of evening wear.

The club had been his own idea. In some excitement he had met me one day to make the plans, what little he divulged of them.

"Today we put our speculation to the test," he had announced grandly. "These months of study may have some use. If all goes well, tonight we undermine a game of chance."

He leaned forward with his most conspiratorial air. "You will be a silent accomplice, a mute witness, one might say. Just wear your most elegant clothes—no stinting on that, and be on time." He disliked the slightest inconvenience of waiting and almost elevated punctuality to a test of character. "As for the rest, just follow me. —And, oh yes," this last was added casually, "bring along a hundred dollars or so."

It was merely all the money that I owned. But his demand had such a knowledgeable tone, such confident assurance of the money's safe return, and, too, contempt for even the smallest hesitation, that I asked no further question and entrusted my savings into his hands.

The club, unlike a public place that has a public look, appeared elite. A sumptuous suite, its long rooms spanned one entire floor of a handsome building, well located for its purpose. One could not pass through merely as he wished or because he paid a token fee to gain admittance. Some special introduction, an entree, was what was needed to keep the clientele small enough and still appropriate to this exclusive setting. Phil produced the card of a devotee, a friend his father knew, and on its strength we were accepted and passed from the foyer on through the door.

Once past that door, I picture very clearly how Phil looked. Within the place that holds the memory, I see his face more sharply, crossing the entryway, looking with such disinterest at all the luxury of the room. He was more erect than ever, seeming taller in the long black line of formal clothes. That careful grooming of the head, the brushed and burnished look about the hair was more pronounced with the further flattening he had managed of forelock and sides. Passing the opulent, crystal chandeliers, the tapestried walls, the thick down of rugs, the beautifully gowned women wandering in a sea of men, he gave scant notice to any of them, while I, in contrast, looked to every side, apprehensive and unsure of my-

self amid magnificence of this kind. He possessed a
singular urbanity, a cocksureness of where he was
going, a nonplussed attitude toward attendants who
took our things or sought to lead the way. In his unhurried but knowing passage through the room he
displayed a superior glance and manner that left me
confounded, realizing as I did his inexperience in
those surroundings.

By then we had arrived in a farther room where a
popular attraction, the roulette wheel, had gathered
around itself by far the most spectators beyond the
group of players. As we edged forward into position
so we could see, Phil whispered in my ear, "First we
watch."

Without further attention to him, I was immediately absorbed in the spinning motion of the wheel.
In the perfect stillness that settled with its lurch forward, it seemed to buzz and clang its way around.
Those who watched its turning tapered off their high
spirits, like drunken revelers sobering for the god
worship which had occasioned the festivities. I felt
the mounting tension in each observer watching sus-
pensefully the outcome of the game; with the throw
of the wheel all seemed to throw themselves, too,
upon the mercy of some precious chance, so eagerly
did their glittering eyes follow its high velocity and
slackening pace. As with a single breath drawn in
precise time, the tension was spent in the sigh that
went up as it stopped, a small part jubilation, a large
part regret.

Turning to Phil, I noticed for the first time his
activity. He had pulled from an inside pocket a tiny
notebook, leatherbound, and now set down into it

numbers, figures at every turn of the wheel, making calculations all the while and imparting to the otherwise absorbing game of chance a new raptness, an added concentration not built upon suspense nor on a wily magnetism.

Some about us gave knowing smiles, winking at one another as though to say: another system maker. A few seemed more incredulous at such open searching for a method, thinking, perhaps, it was indecent to expose to public view a vice some practiced quietly at home. But Phil continued in the face of smiles and smirks, the curious looks and whispered remarks, to make his entries, plot his probabilities, compare and calculate in unruffled calmness. Indeed, this coolheaded, scientific manner caused such interest and amusement that the single-minded absorption in the turning wheel and on the reticence or recklessness of players was broken by this stooped figure, bending in utter concentration over the pages of a leatherbound book.

Now someone came up to the croupier and whispered. They both looked up at Phil and then at me, who looked over his shoulder, nodding in agreement. I intercepted their studied stares and prepared to be escorted out, none too politely, along with Phil. But no, one nodded, one shrugged, one walked off, the other remained. By then it was apparent that word had spread to other rooms that someone was challenging the wheel, was working a system, that something was going to happen, for people streamed by in greater numbers, craning their necks as though in search of someone.

Finally, after sufficient study, the ranks around the

table swollen to twice their former size, Phil commented to me in his most categorical tone, "I have the periodicity. . . . Now we play." This was said loud enough for those immediately behind us to hear, and for an over-all buzzing to begin.

We moved into the circle of players. Phil took out his own money with a libertine air, and took mine with quiet authority over its future. The croupier looked at him with decided distaste. Phil regarded him like some mechanical toy that needed only to be wound up to set all else in motion. The wheel spun, and an even greater hush than before settled over those gathered to watch its course. Some could not tear their eyes from Phil's confident vigil and missed the gyrations of the slowing wheel. In my distraction I could not watch it too long, and riveted my eyes instead on the pile of converted money that was at stake. The exclamation that went round drew me again to the wheel that stopped just then precisely at the number Phil selected. A whispered "Luck!" was taken up by the crowd, but Phil did not notice such externals of the occasion.

All was set as before. Phil consulted the numbers in his little book before placing a bet, while more than ever people whispered and strained to see. Again there was the silent interval, the mounting tension, and, at last, the simultaneous expiration of breath when the wheel stopped with a rumble, halting a second time at the number where Phil had placed our winnings. There was a gasp and the over-all excitement became greater now. There were whispers, rumors, commentaries spreading throughout the room. "He'll lose the third round," someone nearby predicted. "Twice, yes; thrice, no," another voice called sagely from behind. Waves of comment, mostly pessimistic, reached us regarding the next play. "Stop while you're ahead," someone advised. I was inclined to agree. However, there was no hesitation in Phil, who was in charge of the enterprise and who was coolly placing all we had won on a new number that a quick perusal of his notes directed him to play.

Now the excitement had risen to the highest pitch of the evening, as though previously absent had been some sense of competition that Phil's defiant appearance had infused into the game. The spectators divided into separate camps. First, those who rallied about any promise of victory over that flamboyant chance that victimized them time and time again, those, too, amused by blatant challenge to its supreme sway, and others who ardently hoped a system would be uncovered that they, too, might find, to guarantee their own successful future play. Then, on the other hand, there were still others, resentful at this scientific flaunting of that very chance which was their secret love, which, because contrary, unpredictable, unsure, kept their fascination that would wane were it shown to be a calculable attraction. I watched them all, forcing myself, at last, to follow the final contortions of the wheel. It staggered and fell again in place. There it came to rest, unbelievably, exactly on the number Phil predicted for the turn, a third time proved right.

A general uproar broke loose at this, a hymn-singing to his calculations, an amazement at this unprecedented act. People pressed on him from every side, some asking to be told the system, others merely pressing on him warm congratulations, someone whispering in great agitation, "I'll strike a bargain with you."

"That's it," said the croupier, nodding him toward the cashier.

"Three was my limit, anyway," Phil replied, still callously taking his chips, ignoring the questions, promises, and exclamations all around us. He motioned me alongside.

Lionized all the way to the exit, crowded against, called to, even photographed, he accepted all without comment. With a decidedly nerveless smile, he exchanged the chips and, as unconcerned as ever, passed to me a share of what he had won—in my life an unprecedented amount to hold in the hand.

Once outside, in the cold air, I knew the soaring I was too dazed to feel within the Club.

"Do you realize what you've done?" My voice was excited, even hectic when finally revived to speech. "You've only cracked the wheel, that's all! You found the periodicity—just like that." Here I snapped my fingers, and enjoying the sound of victory in the ear, I did it once or twice again, feeling more and more carried away. "Just think, in one fell swoop defeating chance on its home ground . . . imposing order on chaos . . . to justify the faith of all those people placing hope in spinning wheels, believing there is system in it somewhere!"

Phil laughed. "I never doubted *that*. It was another thing entirely that involved the risk."

"Another thing?" He loved being pressed to prolong the mystery.

"It's quite an easy matter for anyone who's made a study of any seriousness to find the periodicity. The trouble is, they never allow it to be done. They change the wheel every twenty minutes or so to avoid just such successes as tonight."

"But they let *you* work it out. Why was that?"

"I had a reason for being so blatant, working it before their very eyes, attracting such a crowd. Just as I thought they might, they saw advantage in having me play and leaving the wheel unchanged. Changing it is for their own protection. . . . But in this case *not* changing it was to their gain. Look what happened in that crowd tonight, what they will spread among their friends tomorrow. Someone—an upstart like me, no less—showed he could work a system. They'll think: why not they? and play more feverishly henceforth. But of course, no matter what they try, it will be to no avail. The management will reinstate changing the wheel—and they will lose, as always."

"You mean our chance of losing was that great—even if you succeeded?"

"I suppose the odds would be discouraging. But, on the other hand, chance is nearly always a fifty-fifty proposition, and nerve can carry you a good way across the other half."

Here he gave a sly smile that slowly spread across his entire face. It gave him a look of such disingenuous pride in his achievement that at sight of it I could not restrain a laugh. Needing only this sign of appreciation, he too burst into laughter on the sidewalk, and together we walked, still convulsed, all the way down the street.

(9)

IN ORDER to honor Phil's partial victory over chance, we had, of course, to celebrate. We were determined to make it a special occasion, a luxurious evening, and met for dinner first, wanting to gourmandize to heart's content.

Drinks had passed from hand to mouth, progressively less sure of journey's end. For hadn't drunkenness as part of old religious rites been long associated with attempts to reckon chance? And so our voices rose, our laughs increased. As one last tribute to the stalwart waiter who glanced at us dismayed with each new round of drinks beyond sobriety, Phil removed, with studied care, five lovely flowers from the floating-blossom centerpiece that graced the table. He arranged each one with dignity atop the wine stains we had lately splattered on the cloth. With great attention to detail, he set afloat among the other blossoms five fresh, crisp dollar bills, each carefully creased and folded, in place of the five flowers withdrawn for other use.

Then we passed into the street with loud guffaws, garrulous for no reason. From time to time we stumbled and had to lean on one another for support. But on the whole we forced ourselves unevenly ahead, no matter how precarious our balance and our step.

By then we had come to a large, brightly lit marquee, a burlesque theater, where huge posters announced the main attractions for the week. Pictures of the stars were generously posted all around, heavily fingered before deposit under glass. While I was pressed almost flush against the wall while admiring the scenic wonders, Phil studied them from several paces back, measuring proportions, forefinger raised in air and eyes asquint, as though he were examining in excruciating detail some unfamiliar work of art.

Suddenly music began to blare, coming not from inside the theater but rising only yards away, where trumpets, tambourine, and drum had started up, followed by voices that joined the demonstration and put the struggling brass to shame. "By the rivers of Babylon" they sang, the drum of indecisive beat, the trumpet faltering on a note, but words and voices ringing clear and strong above the wavering chords. This loud demonstration sent the theater manager rushing from the door to shoo them off, but his presence only spurred proceedings to a higher pitch. Besides, he noted that we abandoned interest in the show, attracted as we were by the noise, the sight of uniforms, the clarions still raised in hymn, and so he left his unsuccessful ranting to turn to us and physically encourage our interest in the show.

Phil shrugged him off, planting himself firmly before the controversial minstrels, where he drew a quarter from his pocket and dropped it loudly into the cup extended eagerly for every offering. His gesture brought a round of near-applause from the delighted group, sulks from the disgruntled manager, as Phil suffered a drumroll and a smile from the lady drummer and a lengthy handshake from the bass. While they still reveled in their moral victory, Phil bowed grandly toward them. "To God—" he indicated the extended cup—"and now, to Caesar," and he plunked another silver piece upon the counter as loudly as he could, for all to see. Now the manager usurped the smile of victory, while the demonstration of instruments and song resumed its musical exhortation once again, this time renewed in fervor for its recent spiritual defeat.

Inside the theater was the most appalling smell on earth. The three contenders for title to that foul smell overwhelmed in combination. Most immediate were odors of rancid food that briskly sold from yellowed cases barely a step across the threshold. Then, from all directions came the fumes of alcohol that settled in new fermentation all through the place. And last, there were, in wide assortment, latrine smells that finally subdued the others, making the nostrils smart in homage to their domination.

We were then at the rear of the theater, accustoming our senses to the change of air and to the prevailing dark. From where we stood, most of the patrons seemed sprawled and headless, short, black hulks, for rows of empty seats predominated in those rear aisles. While we turned bleary eyes upon the theater, the orchestra began its bellows. A dozing drunk in the very last row jumped up electrified at the cataclysmic sound, turning in every direction, frenzied, until, his fears dispelled, he fell immediately into his former sleep, once more slumped over in his seat. The half-empty bottle by his side, seen as half full in our unsteady condition, was gingerly confiscated by Phil, who embraced this symbol of another man's salvation into his open arms.

Then we made our way hesitantly down the aisle, littered with trash so that we stumbled several times. We were only too relieved to slump, like all the others, into a waiting seat.

At last our attention was taken by the sound of heavy bodies thumping and falling all over the stage, while the audience alternately laughed and grumbled at their prolonged antics. They were growing tired of the jokes and rumpus and had started to whistle, even to hoot displeasure. The din mounted. I noticed there was a black, many-legged creature crawling on the bottle Phil had handed over to me. I flicked it off, almost upsetting the bottle, not to speak of Phil, who straightened it with some mistrust in my hand. I looked at the dark flooring and wondered if the whole ground below us might not just as well be made up of thousands of those black crawling forms for all I knew, like sets on stage that were not single-hued at all but composed of countless tiny dots scattered across a solid surface. I raised my feet to the hump of the seat in front of me, and wiped the mouth with the back of my hand before taking a long pull at the bottle.

Some people had started a rhythmical clapping that others joined in agitation. In some interest, I looked about to see who it was that came there. Up in the balcony mostly women sat in small, laughing groups, while up in front men stamped their feet, and some amused themselves with their female companions, running their hands along their arms and necks in anticipation.

The orchestra had stopped its braying and a solo drumroll vibrated through the stomps and shouts. A gradual diminuendo of drum and cries passed into heavy silence as the curtains parted with a slow grandeur. Clinging to the folds of drapes, a mass of feathers, like the soft back of a great, plumed bird with a peacock-spread behind, quivered in the interval of suspense. Then, with a sudden jerk forward, an arm and leg appeared, and the whole body pivoted around to show a sparsely dotted underbelly and a strangely unbirdlike face. There was a cheer, a round of applause, and now the music became limpid and full of drumrolls by turns. The plumed head remained motionless as the feathers rustled, and the underbelly heaved back and forth; the pelvis was overcome with a hypnotic rolling movement arrested by a sudden spasm of stillness.

As she finished, the drumrolls heightened, and her wing seemed to break off, for it was left behind on the floor and her long, white arm trailed in its place. I watched in fascination as it happened again, and the other wing fluttered to the stage, and another white arm replaced it. There was still the plumage behind and on the head, and those speckled places in front. The cheers and applause were sparser now, only a vulgar phrase popped out now and then, with her new posturing. The whole rear part of the body was thrown suddenly to one side before some of the back feathers dropped, and then others, so that the peacock spread was discarded in three separate sections.

Now the plucked bird, her headplume flouncing, moved toward the runway that went off to the side. As she passed, she pushed aside hands that reached toward her, plucking off, as she did so, one of the

speckled places, throwing it into the mass of arms
and hands reaching out for it. She moved on, almost
letting someone take the next himself, but withdrawing just in time to heave it up in the air with a laugh.
There were more hoots, followed by a general silence,
for she was almost completely unclothed now, one or
two speckled places left, and her large head feathers
still swaying. She was closer now, and I saw through
a film her tawdry, painted face, and the little rolls of
fat at the waist. She seemed not to sense any short-
comings, and in the end, she was quite right. It was
the challenge of her walk, the knowing step forward
and back, the conscious undulation of her flesh that
absorbed everyone.

But there was still more to come. The plucked bird
had moved to snatch away the remaining speckles,
and her bare, swollen breasts emerged there, beginning their gyrations, the quickening pendular swaying and the rapid, circular twirl, the sudden reversal
of direction, the slow movement, and the temporary
stop before she began again. I marveled at her art-
fulness, at the centuries-old refinement of those sensual skills, this show of muscular control done with
a technical expertise and virtuosity.

There was not a sound while everyone watched,
absorbed in her final thrust, when, filling the momentary lull, there rose a soft, chortling sound
nearby, a repressed, unexploded well of obscenity
that grew louder, louder, like the half-human sound
of some unseen animal being that projects its pleasure far into the silent desert night. It intruded on
the stillness of the dark theater. The audience, taken
by surprise, turned and leaned to find the source of

that sensual sound. I, too, looked quickly to the side
to intercept the chortle. But all the glances had
stopped to rivet themselves on me! Phil, too, was
staring into my face in some surprise, and in his eyes
I saw with amazement that it was I who had perpetrated that particular indignity at the height of
silence.

Drunk as I was, I must have shown my shock that
the sound that had filled my ears, that had seemed
so deafeningly close, had been my own. Somehow,
though outwardly absorbed with feelings of combined fascination and disgust, that sound had been
lying in me, ready to rise out of my strangely parched
throat and drunken mind. But the fact was that it
had come from me, nonetheless. Some unknown part
of my being had found pleasure in what had repelled
or secretly amused the rest of me. It was strong
enough to find voice to express its relish in that awful chortle that I shrank from in remembering. Or
did I wince at the fearful thought of those unsuspected states that lay sleeping in all of us, that might
overcome us someday with as little warning?—some
small voice that might become autonomous and one
day lay claim to one's whole being. Was it just that
that happened, for example, in those pitiful creatures
possessed of strange words, hallucinatory thoughts,
goaded by alien persons within themselves to some
shocking, absurd act?

But the blessed fuzziness that has long exalted the
drunken state descended over me, and before I knew
it, we had both banished everything from mind as
we laughed, cavorted, and staggered from the theater
into the street.

(10)

L A U R A came into my mind just now. She seemed to look right past me, although she faced in my direction and we were only a few feet apart. She wore a pale yellow dress of some soft fabric that made me want to touch it. She rarely wore yellow, for it was slightly jarring against her white skin, but it was a *pale* yellow, and it seemed right then. There was a *then* once, and in that *then* she sat exactly as she sat on the tip of my eyelid in the *just now* that has passed. Seeking her, my memory has brought up from a forgotten time a replica of that yellow-clad girl staring beyond me to another place, head tilted just a fraction to the right, and her hands, one cradled in the other with fingertips up, in her lap.

And when was that *then*? It might have been centuries for the evocation of a far place and a distant time, or it might have been days, for it was only days ago that I pressed my ear to my grandmother's heart beating in her neck, days ago that I argued with my fantastic Michael for the first time, days ago I found a friend, met Laura. It is as easily one as the other in the unchronicled world of the mind. Does it matter that one is not yet thirty and already inclined to the rumination of an old man?

But I must remember that this rumination began with Laura in a happy time. At least I thought it happy and that made it so . . . Laura complete in face and gesture, the way she looked that day . . . I realize that my striving for her image has been in vain; she can be summoned up intact only if still enveloped in the lost moment that retained her in memory; she cannot exist free-floating, without it. . . . There was Laura in her yellow dress, the dark hair fluffed against her face . . . a long stone bench blanched by the sun . . . enclosed by a green wall of shrubs on three sides, our backs to the red brick of the fourth . . . empty, but for us . . . and the weathered Shakespeare, facing us, off to the side, drab and colorless in his chiseled Elizabethan garb . . . the flower bed at his feet restive with crimson and gold. His watchful gaze persisted through my truncated readings of Duncan, Banquo, Macbeth—a whole roster of his well-known progeny—as I drifted from one role into another, giving line cues, made reticent and bold by turns by the implacable Bard who might have turned the gray of statuary from this experience alone. But he was well used to abuse, and besides, he had no recourse but to stand and glower, for the library had rooted him firmly on his pedestal, inasmuch as it had failed to implant him lastingly anywhere else. Laura had thought of it . . . the library garden where we might be alone together while she ran through her part. She sat there in her pale-yellow dress, her hands cradled in her lap, her presence urging me to read unabashed . . . amused when confidence carried me too far . . . leaning across my arm to see the playbook . . . tapping her finger on the penciled part in sly reproach . . . laughing with closed lips, back in her nose and throat. But by then we were underway, and she never noticed me after that. As she responded with her lines, I let my eyes stray from the page while she spoke in her dark, gentle voice. I saw that she was no longer present by my side, warming the cool bench, but might have been in a distant place as well as there. She looked in my direction but not at me, out at the great beyond where only trees and hedges stood, but where she saw more than the wind stirring. Her face told by its transport what she saw there . . . in its leaning forward, in its small darting movements of the mouth, and that grand effort of articulation in her eyes, become the muted green of shrubs, quivering while reflecting a secret life that took form beyond me . . . the formal clipped bow of a hedge . . . the extended hand of a tree . . . the vigorous shrug of a bush. . . . Her cast surrounded her as I mouthed the words, advancing, retreating in perfect rhythm to the speech, with flawless gesture and rapport. They were as convincing players as she had ever seen, for they were imbued with her own rich imagination, and her face almost colored with excitement. I saw no one, nothing else but the transfigured Laura become Lady Macbeth. So when I saw her live eyes making of the world of hedges and of trees costumed retainers, would-be kings, the walls of Dunsinane and Birnam Wood, I thought it no less strange than that she should be, not Laura then, but a majestic, too anxious queen. When we had done, the book fell closed to my feet, and I could blink away the queen and find again the girl beside me . . . yellow dress and slight smile . . . the girl who came unbidden to mind a moment ago, enclosed in this lost moment, too well-loved to die, but too futile, too late . . . to live again.

But the inevitable day came when sympathetic shrubs became live actors on the stage, each with his own voice, and the confluence of several minds wrought from once-living trees and stone an Inverness and Dunsinane made visible to all. This day, the actual performance on the stage, was, for the actor, a far less critical moment than that other that occurred, devoid of any physical reality save what was created there, in the inner recesses of the mind. This was its execution, the physically made-real; it was the living of it through and the fruition of that other more important, if successful, act. At least this was my view based on the example of Laura who, after all, compared this moment to successful regeneration —what was it?—the word entombed on the page roused to palpable life, Lazarus made whole for all the world to see.

Falling into speculation, I waited with all the others who had gathered for that moment that was at hand. The curtains were drawn, and we, who sat row upon row beyond it, made a noisy, chattering bunch, each one conscious of all the physical trappings surrounding him—his neighbor, his seat, the size of the crowd, another of those anonymous chandeliers lost to memory. The stage might not have existed at all for the attention paid to it then.

My place was next to Connie, Phil just beyond, though they little realized I was of their party, and the unescorted girl to my right smiled up at me pleasantly, thinking I, too, was alone. Phil leaned his head close to Connie while she whispered in his inclined ear, making him smile at the words. I thought how heedless they had become, not only of me who sat there, but of Laura, whose day this was, and who seemed not to count at all in their private whisperings.

Just then the house lights dimmed . . . the room darkened for that invisible alteration that transforms a bustling theater hall into the dramatic experience. The gradual dark obliterated our separate faces, making of us that impersonal whole, the audience. It halted conversation, and all eyes, as one, strained toward that same curtained stage that had not attracted a single glance in the full light of evening. There was a tension and alarm in that silent interval. I wondered what this moment was like back there, in that wilderness of plank and wire still another dimension beyond the stage, where actors stood readying themselves in the wings, no longer resembling their former selves, but not yet called into being by the mysterious white light spreading so magically across the stage.

The play began. A crash of thunder and the eerie play of lightning illumined the darkened stage, and a chill remembrance there was no time to ponder coursed through my taut limbs. I only knew that what confronted us up there, flickering with a ghastly glow, could not have been more real. The light of the storm passed over three stooped figures in the corner of all that barrenness, taunting them to life. Words tumbled from their cracked lips in a semi-coherent stream, rapidly, at a rate no earthly talk could take. And it was done—with this second's brush the underworld, now alight in the wane of cosmic tremors, enwrapped all subsequent events in its unearthly folds, so every place that captured in its contours and details the verisimilitude of the world was prisoner to its secret sway. Thus campsites, stirred by sight of blood and rising shouts of victory, were yet ominous, as though something hovered in the air, like those same shades that had sought refuge in the encircling fog. And in old castles, the same that Scottish lords had made their petty dukedoms, one believed the clang of armor that one heard, and the cold northern blasts that seeped through heavy palace walls, yet all the while that passions flared and spent themselves, absorbing us within that wide inner chamber, one's glance was bidden upward to those cloistered bedrooms beyond sight where men found death beneath their sheets and madness in their dreams. Thus each time the dark sisters reappeared one thought it less strange than before, for one had in the meantime imbibed more deeply the air polluted with their breath.

Through this opaque, contrary world walked Laura, though there was no way for me to know it but for my prior knowledge; even the thinly gleaming printed fact in my lap was invisible to the eye. Understandably, she had to be snuffed out to accommodate this omnivorous creature, who in the resurrecting still retained a touch of ghoulishness, made welcome in that oppressive, subterranean air. Perhaps, too, it accounted for the strange exposure of layer upon layer of her, complex contradictions laid bare that would have been covered over had they attained full life. The feel of velvet seemed newly intoxicating against her skin; at the same time, only an old assurance could turn her 'round so suddenly in defiance of that long, treacherous train. Then, too, she was more queenly not a queen, more rational delirious than in her wakeful utterance, more piteous slaking blood than in her bloodless dream. Everything turned sinister, opposite: peace became raging war, mornings dark as night, prized horses wild and cannibal in their stalls. Through aberration coursed a seam of poetry, a limpid word pressed on a murderous thought. Yet one was carried by its articulation, swept along its inverted truth until one felt as choked as the assassin, as overwrought as the least servant who bowed low, disembodied as that passionate queen, and emotionless as Macbeth.

I thought the clap of thunder had begun again, and darkness had crossed the stage a second time. But strangely, the curtains were in full view, were parting anew, and all that recent carnage stood incredibly back of it. I stared, confused, dismayed; their lively smiles and curt nods seemed more ghastly than the grim evening's host, and the new brightness repelled. At least Macbeth and his dim Lady were lost to darkness—but no, now they, too, reappeared—he tugging at her hand, propelling her along with him across the stage—he bowing far forward, and watchful, stepping back when she did not. The thunder grew; it mixed with cries and shouts, becoming deafening, but she returned a sleepless gaze, a disoriented stare into its face, still regally unbent, disembodied as before, remaining thus until the other's armor flashed and he took her, unknowing, by the hand and out of sight again.

Almost at once the hall was suffused with the simulated daylight of before. One by one those in their seats awakened in fast emptying rows to the accompaniment of snapping seats, dropping programs, and the fitful surge of crowds moving toward narrow exits. In this dazed state, I realized the stage had receded from sight. The part that had absorbed us was curtained off, and though I knew behind the heavy drapes everything stood in the same place as before, it was almost as if they had never existed, so remote did they become in the brightly lit chamber. They were suddenly without coherent meaning, without reason for being, each thing becoming something altogether different, as the proscenium arch seemed now part of the architecture, and the curtains, like the chandeliers and molded walls, part of its decor. Nothing remained of their other significance except in us. And even the people in the auditorium had returned to what they had been, taking up the conversations of before, finding again the thread of their lives that had commingled in the darkness with every other.

I made out Connie, almost in the aisle, brushing the tip of Phil's ear with a kiss, and Phil who smiled at her and ruffled through program notes, waiting for me to rise. Once again, I was aware of their particularity and my own.

"Everyone must have been backstage by now," Phil commented as we walked toward the stage. We mounted the steps and found the opening in the curtains where we could pass inside.

As I foresaw, the field of battle was in view, the gray outside of Dunsinane and the wide open place where shields had parried sword thrusts and bodies fell, fainting from their wounds. But there was only silence now. One could not discern a castle in those painted walls, shabby and paper thin, nor discover the unnatural heavens in the dangling cables and hidden lights overhead. I looked away, wishing I could walk straight into the night air, carrying away, like so many others, the illusion intact, permanent because believed complete. And yet the residue was small; most of it had vanished for them, too.

Through this drab unveiling, my eye found Laura, standing to the side, flanked by three or four admirers, still in her silken nightdress and strange coiffure, lines painted on her face, years added to her smile and eyes. In face and figure, deportment and glance, it was the chilling apparition of the stage, but all illusion had been snatched away for me and true natures laid bare. Gratefully I recognized my own dear Laura, her youth peeping out beneath the dyes, all that was familiar of her caught in that half-melancholy attitude of intense listening and inner distraction.

I rushed toward her, ignoring those who could not drop their compliments at her feet and quietly depart. I covered her hands with mine, surprised they were so cold, impassive to the touch. She responded with a smile, but her eyes only half contained my image, and she worked doubly hard to focus on everything around her. The edges of things must have been blurred, for she looked especially to the outside of objects to keep them fixed. There was something dazed about her, as in those last moments onstage. I held tightly to her hand and remained silent, remembering it took several minutes for me, a mere spectator, to obliterate what had taken place there, to shake off its spell. How much the harder for her, who had been of it.

But Connie and Phil exchanged uneasy glances.
They made light conversation, even remarking on
Laura's tiredness, preoccupation. At last, fully disturbed, they mentioned the party—wasn't she changing now?—it must be quite late. Laura made no
move to rise; there was no offer to don her street
clothes, not even an indication that the dark lines and
chalky powders were not part of her. Her distraction
was so complete that she seemed calm, collected. Only
the extra effort of her eyes to place things showed
the strain. I thought of the contrary world of the
play . . . everything opposite, like Laura now, seeming so cool, relaxed; her poise sharpened to a brief
smile.

"No party?" I asked.

She shook her head from side to side, as though
ejecting some foreign matter from her ear. Connie
began to protest, but I nodded them away, sending
them off to the party with a half-promise, "We'll see."
But I knew we wouldn't go. The parties were not for
Laura, who carried the stage there with her, entering with the harried look of Signora Frola in her
eyes and leaving with it still etched there. They were
for those who could break themselves sharply from
what they had become, set it aside with their costume, rub it out of them with cold cream. Not for
Laura who held the strained reason of Lady Macbeth
in her brief smile.

Leaving the Theater Hall, we walked in silence
across the tree-lined path to the street. People stopped
short to stare at the long-cloaked woman, heavily
lined and powdered, who walked slowly at my side.
For the moment they might not have thought her

of the theater, for there was no glamour in the harsh whiteness of her face. Heads turned to follow her graceful form that took no notice of them or of the swollen traffic of the street. They were all equally unreal to her whose reality was still the eerie world of stale plots and midnight whisperings, that were lost in the hazel confusion of her eyes. Once I saw a greater morbid interest follow us, and I turned to find glowing in the street light the churning motion of her hands that stopped as suddenly as it began. Still wordless, we reached her door.

By tomorrow, I thought as I left her, she will have thrown off her cloak, scrubbed clean her face, and vanquished the spirits that still clung to her. For it was months now that she had been readying herself for this night when the dead would rise for all who came to see, and it could not be discarded in a moment.

The drama had a strange power, almost magnetic, of drawing people inside it. People thought to contain it, but instead it absorbed one after another of them, until it held sway over an entire audience at once. But time was its enemy. Though it could hold hours at bay and muffle ticking watches, its magic properties waned in that same unnoticed time. With its end, those who had cast off time resumed the marking of the hours as strenuously as before. With Laura, who had breathed more deeply deranging potions of air, it would take longer than with the rest. Even in the Theater Hall, I recalled, people returned to themselves at different intervals. By tomorrow its dominion would cease for her as well. True daylight would accomplish that. If the glare of houselights failed to rouse stubborn ghosts, the banished sun would do it. The dark skies winked with lesser planets that covered its whole surface with their glow. Time was their enemy, too. By that same tomorrow that I thought on, these that ruled the heavens, so absolute, so unalterable to the eye, would be set aside as nothing in the bright morning sun.

(II)

THERE is a sense of obliteration in time. Has everyone known it or only I? Something much more fearful than that majestic subjugation of stars by sun, for they reappear to the eye, quite rightly as though they had never left but instead only had their preeminent place usurped for a little while. But what of us? Does some portion of us disappear daily, wafted into the oblivion of sky, never to return again?

I remember once reading out of doors, gradually unconcerned with study as I slipped into an idle dreaming, watching the clouds trail off into nothing . . . mixing into my thoughts other days at school . . . even that most important one when Mr. Allard called me to his desk . . . a stern, even a sadistic man who had the toughest boys edgy in his class, close upon tears with the force of unaccustomed concentration . . . who in a moment of unguarded kindness had called me forward, explaining to my surprise what potential he saw in me, remarking on abilities and strengths I had not realized before . . . the shock of it . . . a jubilant awakening. . . .

For only that, he should have had a cardinal place in my existence. Yet I could not remember more than his name; the man himself was fugitive to memory. Whether he was young or old, slight or corpulent, what he had taught and when—all his particularness was lost to me. Only this vague sense of pastness remained, and this forgotten man and half-remembered act drifting away in it. . . . Perhaps in one year's time or ten, even the moment, the name, would have blown free, that portion of my life sucked like wisps of clouds into the oblivion of time. . . .

Like remembrance of my grandmother's voice that someone in recent conversation remarked upon, saying it was light and airy for someone stout, clear and high when she hummed. And yet I had forgotten it! To think it was among the first to go, as though it never was! A lovely humming she might have started while she worked or continued when we walked. Yet for me it had already ceased to be, long, long ago, even in remembering. More and more of her lay scattered through those clouds that trailed away to nothing.

This other death is as disquieting as the first. These memories that burn more brightly, must they, too, die, and leave us with no sense of specialness at a name, a thought? . . . An empty space that once was full. . . . Discarded parts of us, unseen by our preoccupied selves, dotting the landscape as far as the eye can see, memories slowly shed by our consciousness like the excoriations of snakes that are left

behind to disintegrate in the hot, obliterating sun.
. . . The gradual death, the annihilation, day by day
of what we have been; not all we once were nor all
we have experienced survive the years. But what
does that make of us? Incomplete, truncated beings,
who eventually in old age represent so small a residue
of ourselves that we, the remaining us that has survived, is an inconsequential, fractional part of the
enormity we have encompassed a life long? Do our
lives shrink and shrivel with our shape, so much of
it obliterated in that slipping past of time, there is
too little left to support a special form?

I look back in time, moving from one past time
to another, not knowing what should have intervened, what has been left behind, to make some
memories loom so large and others already seem so
dim. Only, with each encounter with a memory, a
future is mysteriously present in reminiscence. So our
minds, before ourselves, lose track of sequences and
orderings and partake a little of that timelessness that
life opposes and that, fully tasted, is death.

Even as some things lose their particular form,
others struggle into being. How many times have I
set my pen to write again, distracted by a vague stirring in the mind, and found what rustled there
eluded me? It had shape, but not sound; yet if it
was to have a being at all, I knew it was in that in-
accessible sound, if it could be cajoled or coerced
into being. While I strained for the idea, I realized
that within the next moment it could either be
fanned into life or swept along the swift convolutions
of the mind to drown in a bottomless sea. Then the
rustling could become moving lumps, enigmatic fig-

ures, and from that mass of inarticulation sonorous, definite phrases could rise and fall.

It made me wonder how many tiny, unarticulated thoughts there are that struggle to be born, fighting the dark waters that seek to carry them away to oblivion. They are like countless potential lives in spermatozoa that have an unformed vision of life, know only a nameless striving and seeking, and pass away forever unrealized in the fleeting embrace that could have borne them to self-knowledge. —It is too late for most of them; the moment is already past, and who knows whether it was a petty thought or a vast new realm of speculation that was lost in the swift demise of that aborted idea? Perhaps the most productive thoughts and grandest insights of our world were in this very danger of perishing or never being, caught up in the life-and-death struggle of the mind that has occurred every moment of every day through millenia of existence. And it might have been the greatness of such minds that they clutched after the faltering idea, pulled and strained to keep it from going under, and so reclaimed to full articulation what might have been a passing thought.

This process is of great interest to me. In the same way that I grasped at shadowy moments, a music lover can catch at a half-remembered phrase and pursue its characteristic turns and twists until it is the exact one sought for, there being a good chance that it will elude him even then. How much greater, then, is that struggle to trace a thoroughly new and original idea? I can only surmise the task the composer sets himself when he tries to delineate from a general sensation of sound that has besieged his mind the precise pitch, rhythm, timbre, dynamics, and phrasing that account for its individual character— its exact counterpart never having existed before and requiring all known and unknown forces of concentration to put it successfully to paper. Suppose, as his mind fills with a succession and cacophony of sound, he hears one that has never occurred before? Suppose it is an entirely new vehicle of sound that no instrument has yet been called upon to produce and no performer has been prevailed upon to execute—perhaps a supremely subtle rhythmic involution that must be translated from its ambiguous shape in the mind to the scrupulously definite demands of notation.

I have only a glimmer of what it must be—that job of working the vast resources of the mind by the pure ferocity of the will to know. A writer must feel it in those rare moments when that voice comes to him that he knows is his voice, heavily disguised or barely audible perhaps, that is a feeble intimation of what could be his particular writing style, if only it could be understood clearly and entirely in the proud isolation it demands. He must strain as much against its bewitching as its loss, for the ecstasy of perceiving it can be so great that it is rendered meaningless from incantation.

So ideas become or they perish. We await the result, cheated in knowing so little of the struggle. What follows seems minuscule by comparison with the invisible inner raging that, if successful, ends in that enormous first triumph: the possibility of being at all.

(12)

LOOKING myself over, I haven't changed so ter-
ribly much. Once or twice total strangers have
stopped me on the street, recognizing in me the
schoolboy I was. I found it preposterous at the time,
since I saw none of their youthful marks in *them*. But
straining in the mirror at home, I almost saw him
myself, though it seemed strange to have him cou-
pled with thinning places in my hair and more than
a few gray hairs. I expect one day to discover to my
surprise the yellow glow of my scalp exposed to public view, progressively revealing itself until I shall
become more than ever like that earliest self that had
little more than a round gleaming scalp to commend
it to the attention of the rapt world.

The thought of that wretched infant is thoroughly
ridiculous, yet there he is, fully documented in photographs, for posterity's approval, in every momentous
act of his young life—gurgling, bawling, sneezing,
and scowling—and here am I with, granted, not all
worthy but nonetheless thousands of ideas and impressions daily and barely a handful preserved at
year's end. There you have it, ladies and gentlemen,
the judgment of life upon itself. Not by any means to
be sneered at. Were I confronted with the relics of
five years ago, ten years ago—we may stop there or
it would be completely absurd—the blush that rose
would surpass the neon light opposite I so fondly

cursed from my college room.

In those days of invariable glow and wakeful nights, my mind, protesting, turned from that predictable fluorescence to the unpredictable realm of changes about me. This is a subject I have since been so thoroughly concerned with, the thought might escape the reader that I was far less tutored in its operation than I am now. Even this is a demonstration. But not to seem more naïve than I was . . . it is clear I had already posed the question philosophically, one might say intellectually, for myself. Its force and reign had preoccupied me many times in discussion with Phil. What was lacking was a practical understanding in everyday terms. For friendship, so hard won by me, seemed the large encounter, marked as it was by its succession of discoveries, its unexpected windings up the ladder of understanding —all those things I thought change to be. It blatantly ignored the possibility that these most recent learnings, too, would alter, diminish, even disappear.

Here is where that young man of some five . . . is it really ten? . . . years ago seems most naïve. But the lesson of changes has been well demonstrated my life through, and nowhere exemplified more fully than in the Phil and Connie that succeeded the others.

I was convinced the way things went with them was little short of lunacy. Who could have foretold that she would want quite literally what she had asked: systematic withdrawal from all but the rite of their love-making? In my eyes, it was a sophisticated suicide pact; conversely, to Connie, it was the willful annihilation of the outside world, which, though

not a grave sacrifice to her, was for Phil an unspoken
agony of denial. To watch them together was to understand the difference.

Connie stared at Phil in long bursts of frozen wonder. She was like a Narcissus regarding the sullen
image so magically reproduced in shimmering drop-
lets of water; her gaze never wavered. Walking
through parks, she looked neither to the right nor
to the left of her. Explosions of flowers defied in-
difference, but were successfully ignored; the seasons'
changes, if left to her discrimination, would never be
recorded. In short, she accomplished her object, even
thriving in this attitude of obeisance to their union.

Then there was Phil. At times one wondered what
possessed him. He would gaze as absorbedly as she,
and quite suddenly, especially when her glance was
distracted, his eyes would dart out to embrace the
world. His attention flew from one object to another
in furtive haste, storing impressions for the time of
famine when his eyes fed again only on her.

One wondered how long this could go on. Surely
his dissatisfaction could not go unperceived forever.
One day it was bound to strike Connie that the Isolde
myth so precious to her was of her own making, and
that her unwilling Tristan was basically untrue to
his pledge. But no, my prediction remained my own
hollow secret, for as time passed, outward signs of
duress vanished. But I noted one thing: Phil's devotion increased proportionately as *her* strength flagged.
In fact, I watched with amazement the transformation that occurred and made Connie hardly recognizable as the girl of the preceding months.

A summer intervened, so that the difference was

heightened by our not seeing her, and the shock increased. First of all, what had been an infrequent
loosening of the hair had become the daily manner.
No longer was it piled high to form a natural crown,
mysterious in its invisible inner windings. Now it
hung loosely down her back, exposed where it had
been cloistered, turning limp and coarse from the
weight and gracelessness of this new freedom. The
lack of artificial tints that had lent an earthiness before—her high color enough to carry it off—was, in
her altered state, merely drab and bloodless, so that
she had the look of many women who in marriage
lose pride and interest in themselves. She seemed
wholly to sustain herself on Phil, adopting the role
of listener and observer; her eyes, when not fastened
on him, were set in a median, downward plane. As
for Phil, he was all the more aware of her in her
self-effacement, solicitous of every thought and motion, constantly interrupting his remarks with a
glance at her, asking her view of matters she could
not conceivably know about.

I remember seeing them at a lecture once. Seated
a few rows behind them, I could watch them as much
as I liked without their knowledge. But I made little
use of this advantage, for the speaker on this occasion
was a young philosopher. His was one of those closely
reasoned talks that demand, beyond the full attention, a sense of the importance of the effort, in itself
formidable and noteworthy, of expressing each
thought with such precision that the whole is a
logically true structure. In addition, the subject was
"Implications of Probability," one of the most famous
treatises of Stermer, and thus a common topic of his

disciples. My interest was so great that I strained forward in my seat, afraid to let my mind be diverted for even a moment; but unfortunately this was accomplished for me by the youthful speaker himself, who at a key moment left the rostrum to demonstrate a proof on the blackboard. While he wrote, my mind drifted to how Phil and I would have argued over this all afternoon a few short months ago, this hour providing us, weeks later, with material for those long conversations of the past. Then, too, directly afterward, Connie would have rapped the table with her glass, tilting her head like the speaker, finding a somber voice to mimic the manner of the afternoon, mixing the low, clipped speech of exaggerated sobriety with clusters of "if-then" and "thus" summations. It would have been done lightly and we would have laughed a long time. But no thought of that now. I looked over to where they sat, Phil more erect than ever, Connie's head resting comfortably at his neck. He was turned toward her, but at the sound of renewed speech from the rostrum he stirred, inclining his body toward the forceful voice that drew him, while his eyes remained fixed on the inert form pressed against him. There was an intense straining in his face from the pull of those simultaneous yet mutually exclusive acts, a look that resembled most the effort of the deaf attending. I felt a peculiar wrench at the sight, wondering how in a few short months the smallest joys could become confused with pain. The look vanished almost as soon as it appeared, for it had escaped in a brief involuntary convulsion from his most private world, visible momentarily only because believed unseen.

But, like a child, not being discovered, I saw much
I was not meant to see. Besides the public preamble
to their love-making—they had an incredible way of
twining themselves beneath a table, tangled to the
knees—I intercepted clues to their changed relations
and evidence of their indiscretion toward others.
Not that these were numerous or grave, but rather
indicative of a heedless insensitivity that overcomes
many individuals in pairs but aggravated here by the
new imbalance between the parties. For in order to
rouse her, Phil adopted many of Connie's old ways
of amusing herself: joking mainly at the expense of
others, noting their idiosyncrasies in terse nicknames,
banter. It was less natural to him, so less becoming,
but pleasing to Connie because of its conspiratorial
tone. In fact, with their heads drawn close in scur-
rilous glee, an occasional smile lightened her immobile face. This was the only act she permitted to break
their self-absorption. For I saw them at outdoor
cafés, in restaurants, on park benches, looking over
the people who passed by, enumerating their physical prominences or deficiencies, sometimes, though I
only guessed, obscenely. But all had to be initiated by
Phil, who warmed her to it, so even these small
gestures were converted into the pattern of their love-
making. She had willed it that way in her heightened voice over coffee while Laura and I watched,
not knowing what it meant; but once having
launched this program of annihilation through
union, she was will-less, having inflicted hers onto
him, carried by this joint emanation. She made
hardly any effort; inertia slowed her walk and made
her speech listless.

Sometimes I saw more closely how it was with them. Once I unexpectedly came upon them on the steps of a new building. Connie, though more deeply distracted from the outer world, so more liable to distress at our sudden encounter, showed no emotion. It was Phil who drew back in surprise at the sight of me, looking startled and confused. Yet it was he who was the better prepared to meet me, having caught sight of me exactly when I saw him. It was a displaced reaction, similar to the feat of the ventriloquist who relays his voice to the dumb object; yet it showed more virtuosity, being, in addition, wordless. Sharing one will, in Connie's view, allowed her to express everything beyond *them* through Phil. So, after an exchange or two about "this bastard architecture," I saw the almost imperceptible pressure of her hand on his arm. Not needing another sign, Phil broke off our pleasantries with such ease, I would have thought the motion came, unseen by me, from within. It seemed an ultimate victory for the "one will" that I had presumed merely a figure of speech.

Weeks passed when Laura and I saw nothing of them; not even their path crossed ours. Once after such an absence, we saw them approaching, arms entwined, eyes set only on each other. How thin Connie looked! The ruddiness and firm flesh on her face gone, she looked, not like the hardy Thuringian girls who dreamed in the sunlight of night falling and circle dances between steins of dark beer, but like those hard-pressed peasant women whom nature has turned sour. They draw a weary breath gazing at the lovely ridge of fields beyond, and walk trying to shuck off the dry earth that has sucked the spirit

like so much rain water. And Phil, beside her, seemed
like a prop to hold her or even more, like the cool,
clay jug to keep her sweet. But he was dwarfed, too;
for, those active, wide-ranging eyes that had given
him greater magnitude were only small pockets of
light around a lens closed to the world. Those curious eyes, once so restless with thoughts, were stilled
by the weight of one only. The two of them passed
us by, not seeing us, I'm sure—and if they had? But
neither Laura nor I raised a voice to call them; a
whisper would have sufficed, so close were they. Instead we abandoned them to the vacuum of their
oneness, unruffling the space that was theirs by intrusion of that which was all else. On and on they
walked, not unwinding their arms nor untilting their
heads, and we watched, helpless to warn that the
path might take them too far. It seemed they would
walk it to its very end, whatever that might be.

One night when it was very hot, causing me to
keep the window open wide and the shade up, that
same neon light seemed the more unbearable since I
could not shut it out. That night I had the first of
two visits I wish to describe in some detail, since for
me it illuminated those peculiar changes I have been
at such pains to mention.

Past midnight, still not ready for sleep, I was surprised at a knock on my door. Phil stood there, a
little unsteady on his feet, when I pulled back the
door, but he recovered himself quickly.

"Just passing by," he murmured under his breath
but discharging enough of it to indicate he had made
an extensive visit before this one to the local bar.

"Is this where you are now? The room is better,

but how do you stand that light?" He lowered the shade with a jerk, diverting the one semblance of a breeze from my path, but also blotting out the red neon glow that was so objectionable. Then he moved on to the desk to finger the books piled high there and to glance at their titles. Finally he dropped into my patched armchair.

"I'm not all that drunk," he said returning my gaze. "In fact, I'm not drunk at all." It was actually true. He had been drinking in order to get drunk, but unsuccessfully, producing none of the high spirits, heightening of the senses, animation, belligerence, or whatever else he had sought. He was only bleary-eyed sober, tired, and not too well balanced on his feet. Seated, he seemed not to have been drinking at all.

"I haven't seen you for days." He tried to make it seem our lives had remained exactly as before and we with them. I introduced a note of diluted reality.

"More like weeks, I think."

"That was very dry," he laughed. "I've been rather taken up."

"I would say! Is Connie well? It's been actually months since I've talked to her."

"I know you think I'm a fool about her."

"I think nothing of the kind. Anyway, it's certainly none of my business and I wouldn't presume to judge." I was confused and apprehensive, thinking the accusation was yet to be amplified.

"You have no opinion? That's either disappointing or overly discreet. —But perhaps you don't realize I find her quite stupid."

I was dumbfounded and must have shown it on my face.

"I thought you would know that. But I want, in a certain sense, to live with her banality."

"You find her banal—but you like it? You'll have to excuse me, but I don't follow that."

"You find it so strange? . . . Of course you must be familiar with Connie's extraordinary romantic notion to which she is so fully committed? I would call it enslavement, if I didn't, in a way, admire it, too. That, of course, separates her from banal people with nothing."

"But don't you care for her?" I asked incredulously.

"Well, I do, but that's really secondary. It's not the thing that holds me . . . shall we say . . . prisoner? —Let me explain. If one is to make a choice, it must be made consciously, aware of the consequences, as far as they are known." He sounded exactly as he had some two years before, except for the strange context of the whole discussion that made it seem all wrong.

"You remember Amory's lecture on Stermer's ideas? Surely you do . . . that place where he defined the increasing limitation of choice? You remember, you begin with a wide range of choices, from among which you are theoretically free to choose. But, once having chosen, those open for the next choice are limited by just so much more because of it, and so it goes for each one after that until you are left with one only . . . and then none.

"In any case, a while back I made a choice that makes this one—of staying with Connie—more or less inevitable. If I take it, my life is set in another direction entirely from what I might have foreseen.

—But that other choice, you see, is already made: I must be committed to something."

He made this declaration and paused to ready another cigarette. I continued to look at him blankly.

"It's very interesting, in this connection, to compare the present with the past. In the 'thirties, let's say, people had to be committed, too. The pressures build up inside—for something in all the nothing—and outside, from society, too. —In those days, of course, it was possible to turn it to politics, and feel that the sense of engagement was not wasted, and might, in fact, be converted to a real improvement of the world. It could be directed then because everything did not seem so thoroughly preposterous. Could anyone today make such a decision of commitment honestly . . . thoughtfully . . . intelligently . . . without the grossest sort of self-delusion and world-ignorance?

"But nowadays the need for some kind of commitment is just as great. But one seeks trivial ends because he senses the underlying absurdity, even of this. In rejecting larger forms, we are less deluded, less stupid. —Here Connie fits into place very well. She herself is basically trivial . . . I have to say it . . . but she has, strangely enough, a very real commitment to an outmoded, not to say pretentious, grandeur. Choosing *her* and this outlandish ideal of love would have to mean thorough engagement . . . as you have probably seen. But, you see, to a completely trivial end. What could more suitably meet my specifications?—and what could be more absurd?"

Hearing it exclaimed with such perverse conviction, I recalled thinking he had been undergoing a growing, and at last a total, passion. And, as much as anyone, he had. My mind went back to the time I thought Phil had outwitted chance only to discover another layer of experience entirely had absorbed him.

In reply, I tried to express, as best I could, my vague understanding of the philosophical stalemate forcing him to seek commitment, engagement, whatever he called it. After all, hadn't we both agreed the first day we met that it was hardest of all to live without it? I could certainly not question his statement of finally capitulating to this need, as I was sure it was hard come by. I would merely accept *that* as, for him, necessary and irrevocable. All right then, but this second choice built on that one was unworthy of him, a willful suicide, if that was where all his thinking had brought him.

"I don't believe in suicide, but I don't *not* believe in it, either. You see, that is one of those larger choices that is all the more meaningless. —No, this decision suits me best, and my choices have narrowed, after all."

What could be done with him? He drifted off onto other things, momentarily eager to talk, since it was something he increasingly denied himself.

When the door finally closed behind him, I could think of nothing except of that Phil in the doorway of the Aquarium who speculated on a way of life built in the manner of hypotheses, where failure ceased to matter except to force a new beginning. He had an incorrigible pragmatic streak, sure to press him to a narrow ledge. I was disturbed, too, by the dilemma in our lives he had tried, imperfectly, to articulate.

(13)

I LEARNED something more of Laura the one time I met her father. He was on holiday from school, playing the opposite part of parent journeying to the home of child. He was already there, in what had become, to all intents and purposes, Laura's home, sitting, while Laura stood, in the small living room the landlady had set aside for her tenant's use.

I had not known of her parents, just as she heard little of mine. We were reluctant, Laura and I, to speak about the very things that were most infused with meaning. To speak of them at all and not convey their substance, that being which makes them most personal of all relations, most foreign to universal utterance, was to trivialize them. Those loves and pains that flow between consecutive blood rivers pass from one repository to another; back and forth, they, adjoining generations, replenish each the other. Who can tear them from their beds, preserve intact their substance, which, like life itself, cannot live separate from the secrets of the heart? And so we kept unfashionable silence with regard to them . . . our parents.

Now I knew she had a father back in the small town she had come out of one day, for which she harbored no homesickness or enthusiasm but no revulsion or acrimony, either. It had just been her home that she had had no occasion to speak of.

Now here was her father sitting across from me, watching me with a pleasant smile but making no effort to speak when he had nothing to say. He had heard Laura talk of me before I had arrived. Those were his words upon introduction, and he had gleaned from what little she had said the growing closeness of our relation. For he had drawn back in his seat to regard us both with quiet, blue eyes, glancing at me especially, as though I were a new force to be reckoned with in both their lives.

Laura looked a good deal like him, though what was similar was hard to place. When there is a marked resemblance between father and daughter, or brother and sister, the differing sex often transforms identical traits, so they are not transferred intact. Only after a prolonged search did I discover the eyes set in the same deep troughs and the mouth full in the same place. I saw the seed of Laura in him, though it had long since passed from him to become the mature girl at his side. I felt very humble then and warm toward my own parents, for generation encountered in its wide leap from face to face seemed strange and wonderful. Seeing the years between them, it was amusing to see how Laura asked after his health and habits with the solicitude of a parent addressing a child newly returned home. The irony grew out of the reversed role that occasioned this visit—he, petted and fussed over, to be made comfortable so he would not feel strange, the way parents are with grown children come back to them for a few days. Her father smiled, supporting her undue concern, and one saw that he loved her very much, was gentle with her and perhaps overindulgent. I thought we two had much in common.

While Laura went to class, we stayed to talk until her return. He spoke in an unhurried drawl, paced very slow for me, but I listened the more intently for its hush.

"You must be a few years older than the boys and girls I teach—Laura's age. I remember your high-school generation very well. You know, each group has its own stamp when you've taught a long time."

I thought of the students nowadays and wondered how that soft, gentle voice would reach them. It seemed of another time, when life was more placid and unrushed. It was a voice unused to firmness, not authoritative, direct. All the same, in a very small room, up close to him, it was pleasant and kind, enfolding one.

"You are twenty, twenty-one. And have you never been to war?"

He said it as though it explained something about me, perhaps some unformed quality, though his meaning was not clear.

"No," I answered, confused under his gaze.

"But your father was . . . or, was he not *ripe* enough for *his* war?" He smiled at the turn of phrase. Even hard humor was made gentle in him.

"No, he never went to war."

"He was a lucky man, and so are you. To have lived so long and been only in the shade of war is a blessing . . . though war touches everyone close enough."

He sighed and fell silent. They were so very sad, those two. I saw the melancholy stretched across his blue eyes, and recalled how it flickered, too, through the haze of color I knew in his daughter. Such a melancholia of spirit gripped them that it made those with them weightless by comparison. I saw it the more clearly in Laura while I watched it in him.

"They don't seem to understand, the young ones I teach, that there is such a thing as war, depression, hard times. They read their books and learn their lessons, but it passes over them as though it never could be. —I was like that, too, I guess. Unprepared at eighteen to brush dead bodies in the grass and hear the sounds I heard. —We'd like to help them to know . . . before . . . we, teachers, parents; but we never get through, somehow."

"People learn soon enough, if they have to at all," I replied, trying to sound as knowledgeable as he. He looked at me with interest beyond the moment, and I felt shy and uncomfortable.

"Perhaps they do." He retired from the scene to await my move.

"Did you come alone?" I asked.

"Did Laura never tell you—about . . . us?"

"She seldom speaks about herself." I tried to retrieve what seemed an error, but he let it pass, unruffled.

"It's very painful for her . . . home. —Her mother is not living, you know."

"Oh, I'm sorry."

"She died—only a few years ago. I sent Laura away to school. It may have helped some."

It grew on me, hearing only this much, how little I knew of her. I glimpsed Laura as a girl only when she described herself in her earliest costumes, with a

will to act. I thought of her, too, in the snow, looking so small, and I not knowing the past in which to
place her. Each knew few facts about the other, but
our indefinable parts had met and were well ac-
quainted.

"I would like to tell you one thing or other, seeing
that you are Laura's . . . friend. They are personal
things to me . . . and to Laura, too. But I want to
share them with you, since you seem not to know."

I felt apprehensive and excited, as though he were
about to cast aside the enigmatic and elusive haze
that enwrapped Laura. I wanted and did not want to
hear. Her ineffable side seemed more than ever precious to me when I thought it in jeopardy.

"Laura's mother was a fine woman and would
have made a good mother—had she been able. . . . I
don't know if you know how some women become
ill after childbirth . . . mind-ill and incapable, as
Sara did. All the years we hoped, Laura and I, that
she would grow less depressed and helpless. But it
stayed, up to the very end. Finally, when Laura was
already grown, she took her own life and ended the
unhappiness herself." His eyes were paler now than
before, straining to hold back the lifelong flow of
memories unloosed in those few words. But he turned
instead to me.

"It's inexplicable . . . the twists and turns in life.
Sara, healthy, happy, so eager to have a child . . .
and never enjoy it. —But Laura was a loving child.
In her way, she gave her mother much joy . . . as
much as she was able.

"You know, the first scenes she ever played were
for her mother. Sara loved it best in costume with the

props laid all about. She ran to her place and clapped
when we were ready, and she giggled when Laura
came in, in her fine gown and feathered hat . . .
that little thing, not more than five or six, she the
grownup, her mother the child. It was her only entertainment, Sara, watching Laura play-act just for her.
Once, when Laura begged her to take part, she took
the cloak herself and threw it on her back. She cried
with it over her arms, and Laura cried, too, never
asking her after that.

"She died just before Laura went off to school
. . . four years now. . . . If she never thinks of
home, it's just as well . . . for she's a good girl,
Laura is."

He had finished all he meant to say. By his nod
he showed he felt his confidence well placed. He required only that, needing no reply.

I saw that he was a slight man, though he had
seemed taller. I knew now that the tinge of sadness
emanating from him everywhere was braced by a
placid strength. One looked at him and one knew he
had endured. What I did not discern at once about
his classroom manner was apparent now. Just *that*
kept his students quiet and respectful to his slow,
hushed voice. For the one hour each day they saw
him, he could anchor all that restless youth that
floated into him from the shoals to sit at his tranquil shore.

Even *I* left him unburdened, though I knew despair would settle upon me the farther I withdrew
from that peace-giving, stoical gaze. Then the
thought of Laura would come, a small Laura, bearing what she had borne with a magnitude of silence.

The feeling would steal on me, too, as it still does, of the little I knew of all the dark, unrecited sufferings embedded so deeply in the lives about me. To the right and to the left, in the least-known and best-loved, there was this invisible chasm, so blithely assumed not to exist, because it was unseen and unexpressed. Yet it was there in everyone, if we could know it.

(14)

THERE is a second visit I had with Phil several weeks after the one previously described. But first, to set the scene, consider how we nonchurchgoers spend Sunday morning. We rise late, weary from Saturday's ease, not expiated by confession from weekend infractions. We seek news of the world, but it is late, and our Sabbatical neighbors have been there before us. On to the next newsstand, farther from our small domain where the T-shirt and sneakers have felt no contemptuous glance. We consider that it might be unworthy of an expedition, this quest for news, for how much could change since yesterday's newsprint? But one never knows. Some stupendous report might appear only in the Sunday news, and we, at the next social encounter, not yet aware of it. Besides, the thought of the day without papers sprawled over the floor, and with the crossword puzzle not done is unthinkable. What would one do in its stead? Meals are staggered with a long

stretch between that is half consumed by this obligation toward the week's events.

We are now in familiar territory. A friend lives
just down the street, he, too, unchurched. Perhaps
he might enjoy sight of a familiar face as much as
I would . . . or perhaps not. But he might also be
looking glumly at the church-directed world, reflecting there to be an unnecessary gap in his daily life
because of Sunday . . . everywhere set aside, estab-
lishments closed, streets silent. What a false sense of
change in a continuing stream of sameness! That
makes us bold. We mount the steps. We knock. We
will block out Sunday, after all.

It was Phil's door I rapped on, and he who opened
it. He was still in faded pajamas but had slipped into
heavy street shoes to let me in. There were newspapers everywhere—on chairs, over the floor—and
little piles of clothes remained where they had
dropped, outlining a path to the bed. To this disorder
was added Phil himself, still groggy from sleep. But
he gradually revived through potions of black coffee
he poured into himself.

The room was in semidarkness; the shades still
drawn against the light. The objects most illumined
and, too, strangely ordered, were the ivory chessmen
set on a small inlaid table in one corner of the room.
The sparse light slipping in at the edge of the shade
diverted one's gaze to them. They were handsome
things, tall, elongated figures with sharp inclined
planes, nevertheless delicate in ivory, but heavy and
forceful in black. We sat near them, which made our
conversation hard to attend to, since I was increasingly drawn to that ivory glint only yards away, long-

ing to touch the cool surfaces, feel the modeling, examine each piece. In fact, from simple admiration of their distinctive carving, I was impelled to set them in motion, permitting them to resume once more their centuries-old rivalry over the same, prescribed course.

Thus we began to play, and the day closed in around the four edges of the board. A world sprang up around the shrouded figures and the lithe, bright ones. Between them, they seemed bent on dividing a small domain, but each side reserved the greater portion for itself. The battle progressed with long, uninterrupted sieges, heavy losses, sharp reversals in fortune, and an unyielding desire to vanquish or be vanquished. At last, the black commanded, reveling in its dominion until capitulation was complete. Then the dark forms and the light returned to their ambiguous places opposite, until their contention began again with the first incursion against their armed peace.

By midafternoon we talked again between long draughts of beer. We ranged over many things, but never touched the substance of our last visit, when Phil had come from heavy drinking to my door. I saw it had been talk tempted on him by an unloosed tongue. He would confide anew only in his own time in his own way, by design, not accident. Her name was not mentioned once the afternoon long, until, finally, he remarked that she had that weekend gone, almost forced by them, to relatives. When he spoke, it was a discordant mixture of pathos and resentment.

"You know, I would like to leave Connie—if I could."

Somehow, out of our old intimacy stretched over hours, he found he could talk again of things not even formulated for himself.

"I think I finally understand the myths we think we know so well . . . Orpheus, so bold, undeterred by hell itself, yet overcome by a simple, vain cry of neglect from Eurydice's lips." I respected his silence as he thought the idea through. I watched the second hand of his Swiss clock go round, full turn, ten times before he continued from before.

"And Psyche, too. . . . All those impossible feats, assuming the greatest risks. But she was held longest by the first sight of tears, pain and affliction. —Yes, Kierkegaard said fears undo ordinary men . . . the exceptional are chained by compassion . . . and it's true." Even at this moment of relative uncalm, he maintained his seriousness and grave honesty in footnoting an idea not wholly his own. No more was said of it. I understood the bitter scruple that made him linger beyond his wish.

I preserved the bond, yet isolation, of our minds by rejoining the stillness and in leaving, soon after, with the silence intact.

(15)

F o r a long time I could transform before my eyes Laura's well-remembered face into the piquant mask of a child. Uncanny how, once it was so vividly suggested, I could imagine the same features I had grown used to in different scale. She who had had no past whatever had suddenly acquired a fixed position in that distant time. There she stood, in the archway of my mind, her present face scaled to a smaller frame, eyes too old to darken a child's face. With weary effort she draped a cloak about her thin child's arms and with extraordinary control thrust herself forward into the adult world in a vain effort to amuse. But this ability to conjure a small circle of pastness on which to implant her present form slowly diminished, just as reflection on what her father revealed to me in confidence was absorbed from conscious thought. It was as though, since one could not maintain a moment of heightened experience too long, a careful curtain of oblivion tightened around it, shielding it from imperfect view and partial, truncated meaning. Thus, peaks recede and are even shut out altogether, to permit us to resume the blind, everyday course of our lives.

Coming for Laura late one afternoon, I was directed to the roof where she had gone with the landlady's daughter. Apparently, each day before her own mealtime, the child climbed to the roof to feed the waiting birds.

Upon slipping through the screen door, I saw them —Laura and the small girl, and that large band of quarrelsome pigeons that remained to feed on whatever scraps had been left them. They were not the least aware that someone had turned on them the same devouring gaze that they lavished on the clustered birds.

There on the roof one overlooked the adjoining buildings and could walk about its flat, black surface, around chimneys and vague protrusions, as though it were a treeless park. One woman across the way was picking clothes from the line, finally disappearing with her basket through a door. Further down, a lazy cat lay sunning itself, heedlessly close to the roof ledge. A green kite, left standing on end and secured to a post where its young owner had deserted it for the day, strained at its fetters to join the wind. They seemed peculiar places, those rooftop parks that dot large cities. They were ugly and full of an invisible sediment that settled on them, but they gave one, nonetheless, a sense of breadth and space, the feel of the larger whole which one lost sight of down below.

My gaze was deflected again to the little girl who audaciously held feed in her hand and called the pigeons by name, wanting their beaks to prickle her palm. The child advanced toward them and Laura swooped down, hugging the girl gently at the waist to restrain her.

"You're already late for supper, you know." Laura pressed the child's head against her skirt, and they half rocked back and forth together in the same place. A real child at her side and a warm, loving smile on her face, Laura seemed at last to throw off completely the diminutive frame I had devised for her. She was a woman who could herself become mother to a child, repairing in nature's way the cruel inversion perpetrated throughout her early years. The thought became almost a wish as I watched there . . . that kind of life for Laura and me. For myself, I had put again into proper order the troubled sequence of the last days, returning to their natural succession the present layer and the past.

But now I saw she pressed the child to her overlong, robbing the gesture of the spontaneity of the maternal embrace. It was, rather, as though she held the child imprisoned, and let pass into that small being something of herself, releasing more and more of her own identity to become one with the child.

An irrational jealousy spun me round. . . . The sound of waves, distant enough to be my pulse, smooth texture of sand, dry weeds moving in the wind. . . . That peculiar sense that she had not been there. . . . A momentary constriction, but then, the wonder and mystery of it—becoming so thoroughly one, I could explode into the greatest consciousness of myself, while she so subtly merged into it as to almost disappear. . . . Perhaps it was the woman's part. . . . Yet a troubling void in retrospect, that absence of other. In a way, I had searched for it a lifetime, and found it quite ultimately there on Pavilion Heights. . . . Still, there was something disconcerting. That way she had of dissolving into my being, far from an impersonal thing, had to be most personal of all, not duplicated in any other experience, absolutely unique. . . . But then, how could there be any question of that? It had been too perfect, too memorable. . . . The moment stirred to new life, lifting me with it out of the shroud of memory—the Pavilion—being drawn to one's fullest height and spanned as far as one could go. Then, at that very moment, being joined by some invisible part that carried one farther still, beyond bounds of imagination . . . free . . . its being different in her, seeming almost more intoxicating for that. . . . The highest order of pleasure that existed seemed to be that delicious abandonment, that ecstasy of fragmenting and dissolving herself, until nothing of her was left that was not reduced to me. . . .

Before I knew it, Laura and I stood alone on the rooftop, just we two together. The child had long since disappeared, had run out behind us, perhaps at that very moment they had first spied me there. And the pigeons had quite suddenly scattered, scurrying hastily in all directions into the air. All I knew was that we two stood pressed together there, while my arms spanned her, found the firm arc of her waist and the deep corrugation in her back.

Above our heads a flock of seagulls had begun to circle around and around, choosing just that place to swing into position, gliding across the sky in their wide, sweeping arcs. They swung past in a perfect loop, unexpectedly changing formation as they turned. Each gull fell degrees lower or soared the smallest bit higher, so it seemed that a prearranged signal called the turns as they swung around again and again, repeating their skilled, slightly altered performance a dozen times or more, each loop precision-perfect, orderly as a drill.

When they had gone we watched for a moment the inactive city. Beneath us people walked and shouted, plates rattled, dogs barked; a restless energy announced the end of day. We, on the rooftop, sensed little of that. Only the geometric splendor of the near and the far city reached us. We stood above it, straining upward into the wide sky, like spires, monuments that leave the earthbound patches to their vaunted mortality. We aspired with common gesture and single breath to that defiant centrifugal force that could disperse us skyward. The wind rushed

against our warm bodies that were lashed together
to form a single, lonely obstacle to its unlimited sky-
path. And high above the city, I thought: we are
young, alive, and it is beautiful.

(16)

THE Fourth of July has never been drab. When
we were children, policemen came early to block off
the streets, flags hung from every window, and we,
already impatient and bored with summer vacation,
cheered at the first sight of old uniforms lining the
street. We clapped before the band came and grew
still as it approached, stirring us with the drumbeat
and clamor. We put our hands to our hearts when
the flag passed or raised our fingers to the hairline in
imitation of old veterans in faded uniforms at our
sides. Most of all, we longed to march ourselves,
along the perfect columns of swinging arms and deep
strides, growing more insistent as row piled upon
row for blocks at a time. Then came the armored
cars and the grim-faced men within, their medals
gleaming and ribbons fluttering across the chest. We
ran and pushed our way alongside, abreast of the
marchers for blocks ahead, rushing to meet the passing of colors three or four times again, drawing out
the parade as long as we could, until we were hoarse
from cheering and tired from excitement and crowds.

In later years there was always the argument:
should we stay home or should we go away, battling

the traffic two long hours to reach least crowded resorts? And if we went, it seemed always longer than that, and there were always fights on the road with the cars piled one behind the other and hot tempers inside them.

If we stayed home, we packed our lunches and walked several blocks to the best park. There the small flags were set in the flower beds, one long border in the garden, and a large, flapping one stood on the platform where a small band was playing patriotic songs and some people sang. Chairs were set in a semicircle all the way around, and from there to the far side of the park, where tables lined the outer paths, people stood or sat, watched and listened. Children ran in between, and families spread out their outdoor dinners unmindful of strangers who faced them at the same table.

Best of all, if we stayed until it grew dark, the band moved through the paths, winding its way to the other side of the park. People walked along the grass beside the marchers in a swelling parade. As if a Pied Piper were leading them, the children ran first from the tables, and their parents, and everyone else in their wake, pressed close behind them, emptying the chairs, the benches, the blankets; everything in sight joined the gathering pilgrimage. When they reached the far side of the park, the band played and the anthem was sung, the wide lawns soon overflowing, for still others came. Those at the back pressed against those in front, the better to see. People jostled and pushed until a hush settled, and the first flare went up. The color spattered the sky, bursting into brittle sparks that shot up and dropped again onto the air. As one faded, a new jet was sent up, new colors spraying the dark sky. The stars were out, and the sputtering, flaming thrusts seemed aimed at their pallid, unchanging glow. A new *ah-h-h-h* rose as white sparks danced over resplendent reds, and both dropped, exhausted into the ground. Children were lifted high to see, but the geysers of color and sound climbed high over their heads, the brilliance visible from even the empty chairs, abandoned tables, and unattended benches that had been crowded before.

How many times I stood in a city park at the edge of the spray of lights, ending with this fanfare the long, busy day! They differed, these celebrations, but remained the same, too, from one city to the next, one year to another, spanning even the change from the boy's view—great, intent eyes—to the duller gaze of the man—the same eyes, still eager to see. Of them all, the best was when I watched from the back with Laura, enfolding her hands, as a cascade of mixed tints flew to the sky. She jumped at each new explosion, and brushed my face at spectacle's end, when she had grown tired. The band, in a tight cluster, finally dispersed, and with that signal the crowds spread over us, moving on every side, we, unhurried, flagging behind. Now and then we saw a familiar face and smiled. Off to the side we even caught sight of Phil and Connie, who must have been farther toward the front, mixed in with those other attentive faces. They were carried away by the stream of people overflowing the paths, covering the lawns. A glaze seemed drawn over Phil's face as they walked, Connie's arm over his. It was not only the effect of knowing what I did, for even Laura saw that he looked more than ever strained, overextended.

We walked the blocks and blocks to her door that Fourth of July, laughing, bending to kiss along the way. We were never happier. The day that began with a picnic, a long walk, this evening spectacle, was finally ended. All the excited, bright holidays of the past seemed niggardly compared to this one. The sense of completeness, fullness Laura brought me made it an unequal contrast. I felt stretched beyond my length, stronger than the strengths of my whole lifetime rolled up in one. I thought: God only knows what I am capable of! Love amplified our shadows while we walked and made the world seem small. My whole life long, like this day, might be one long celebration. I crept between the sheets of my bed, wishing she might always be there. I slept fevered with dreams, hoping never to waken, or yes, to jump up awake, to touch again and know their reality!

(17)

I OFTEN wished I had seen Phil again. —The strange alchemy of time that makes some friendships ripen through all the years and others slip somehow away!

Nothing marked that quiet, retrieved Sunday as a last meeting. And yet it might well have been, for the brief encounters following were little more than bare greetings and casual exchanges, and could hardly be counted. The last would have to be more worthy of remembering, and be sparked by the intense essence that characterized our friendship from its earliest days.

One day he disappeared. With scant regard for anyone, I thought, he had run off. There was no explanation, no farewell, not even belated communication weeks later—only this fleeing, and the questions left dangling in our minds.

There was Connie, leaving school, not finishing, but I saw she would recover—no doubt painfully, but still, she could withstand the wreckage of her dream, the blow to pride, and in the end she would revive again the false ideal that had brought her so near disaster. Had Phil seen she would survive it, at last? Had he known he would do it just that way? . . . Or did it, rather, happen, as it often does, almost without our knowledge of the next act? I could conceive that planning of one course, the taking of another. Were we, then, quite unpredictable natures, truant even to ourselves, finally unknowable, in the most basic way, to our own mind? Was this what marked the world, the whole universe—each scrap of life complex, contrary, teetering this way and that, not knowing its own end? As would be fitting for Phil, he covered the ground he left seeded with speculation. In such a notion of the world, Phil corresponded to my abstract view of man, a child prodigy somewhat comically bent on an impossible mission of mastery over techniques always beyond his present means, ludicrously trying to outwit his elders with a resourceful stubbornness and invention, that enable him to succeed occasionally, even in the face of seeming improbabilities.

He might almost be personally present, though unheard of all the years. For one thing, I absorbed the very best of him into myself, able to resemble what I remembered and admired most more freely in his absence. Then, too, he has survived what afflicts even the best friendships, leaving them scarred, misshapen, with only half their former luster. Between close friends, estrangement walks close by, widening growing cracks. The two have taken from one another, growing similar in many ways, ideas consubstantial between them, similar-textured. This pressure of familiarity can drive them more and more apart, until they have exhausted one another, taken what was new, dissimilar, and used them up, the best things, unknowingly, in transit. Ensconced in the other being, the friendship loses a flexible part, and steadily dwindles, grows stale, turns sour, its best side submerged in the new estrangement.

It may not have turned out thus with Phil. Yet who knows? Were not the best friendships as close as ours, and weren't they, years later, shades of themselves, ruined and shabby?—and they, too, seemed once enduring.

Perhaps we are lucky, then. Our friendship left us still discovering, exploring. It stands fresh, full, and sharp in memory. We need never meet again to have renewed, perfected, what grew between us.

It was well worth a flight if it meant that he was reabsorbed into the mainstream of his life, able to throw off the annihilation that waited to swallow him. A life like that preserves itself, after all; it does not will its own death, however much it may seem to. Through ignominious flight, it may restore its natural life. From the wiser present, I think of his escape as that of some wild, rare, dark-plumed bird that eludes its capture. In one sense, the loss for those that see is incomparably great; but in the end, sight of those wide, multicolored wings stretched skyward is compensation enough.

(18)

F o r a summer beyond preoccupation with Phil, with Connie, beyond Phil's sudden flight, beyond even the deepening love we had already found— Laura and I—beyond them was the summer we had together, every day. Together we saw all and nothing. Rare if the most routine acts of living were not passed in common, we attended, without the knowing, each day's invisible bridge from day to dark.

A summer, all hopes met and then compressed into a limit of time. The succession of days the texture of eternity, yet so brief. The folds of life, each crease seen close. Yet loving is not seeing ends; all becomes the closed structure of each separate day, each one precious for its familiar side, what habit has bred into it, what it can from its start be expected to be.

She was the frame around the day—the sun one saw on waking, still there unnoted, unwatched through afternoon, her pale reflection the last sight I shut my eyes upon to close the day.

What could she wear I had not seen? I knew what green exerted upon the eyes, what yellow wafted into

the hair; where one was worn before and when another; if it were new, if old, if mended. I knew each
thing she owned, revered each for its specialness.
All her tastes were known precisely. If food were
brought, I knew which would be taken, which left,
could choose myself what she would have, and savor
my own meal less pleased than she.

She had the softest voice; pitched low, it spoke
gently, somewhat the way her father phrased words
within and then quietly let them drop. Often I inclined to hear her speak, loving that bending forward
the more because it had impressed on it her manner,
and over it lay my response. When she was more excited, the darkness lifted from her voice; the thin,
high sound of a reed, it, too, grew dry. And when
she laughed, it passed out in the briefest rolls, with
larger silences between.

She curled in the refuge of our love. Most comfortable in the curve of the side beneath the arm, she
lodged there as though it were the inmost bough,
only there protected from the eye of strangers, the
glare of worlds. Stretched like that, she could stay
questionless, without a word, and hours could pass.
Together we had discovered silence and conquered
stillness.

But there was, too, the faceless love that we gave
form. Its silent sway would pass to choose a shape,
some guise that love had been before. Ardent, eager,
we were star-crossed, impetuous in love, defying
hours, in race with time. Quickening with petty fears,
resentful of even the smallest exclusive act, thoughts
given over to times outside the common life, we were
counterparts of Moorish distrust and anxious puzzle-

ment. Nilelike, she could fill with ancient female cunning, and correspondingly I might pass from strained old love to confident, brash replacement. All their Bardic faces placed side by side made the total shape of love. It slept faceless in us until roused to take their universal forms, urged first because it was a natural thing to fashion vapor, and then because it passed into our idyl that now dormant drama which Laura loved, assuming those successive shapes in which I could have a corresponding role. It was the way love in us performed the game.

Her variety remained within, but what was constant spread out into the room we shared that summer. In muted colors, all of spring, she slipped into the pillows, about hangings, into flowers, ferns; something invisible of her reached into each, enough to make a bare and undistinguished place a lovely corner of the world. Disturbing nothing, she infused all secretly in the adorning. As with her person, I found that I might rest my eyes on any part and feel its quiet force. The blinds were drawn halfway against the sun; each move into the outer world was stepping from the cool and beige into the brilliant day.

We went abroad, and something so simple as a walk was more delight—better than solitude, yet like it, too, for all our senses joined to act the part of one. The world was made a fuller place for this collusion. With both our minds and senses, we sought to ferret out the whole, the wide and sweeping part, the broader curve with mine, with hers the smallest bits of life, obscure and hidden things. I saw with her eyes as with my own the world a man could look upon. Our rhythms that rose and fell in separate chambers, each full and various, were made to coincide. She was my complement. In her, I found my other part at last, that being who joined the world and me.

What can I say of such things? What do I know? —Only that one person alters enough to become another. Transitions, meanings, what are they while we live them? Afterward, they never count. What remains is what was and then what has become. Between them, the vast becoming is subtle, unrecorded, the haze. First, the soft, living, palpable one. . . . Laura, the free-flowing shape, the essence that coursed her. With a million eyes, a million ears, a subtle, comprehensive understanding, with a power all-pervasive, even in my most wild, perverse imaginings could I ever have been prepared to go from that loved Laura to that other who stood that awesome day . . . is it still indelible, relentless, in the mind? . . . She, at summer's end, transfixed, riveted, bewitched, before the mirror, no longer of the world, lost in her own? And yet, had she not stood the very first night we met, half-Laura, half-lined, wrinkled —Signora Frola not yet erased? Was I not forewarned, given every evil portent, everything proclaiming madness . . . and yet, did I not think the whole world shared it, everything ambiguous, multifarious, contradictory, complex? Has anyone in all the world been led so unsuspectingly to confront so cruel and shattering a moment? Memory . . . that makes us curse, damn, tremble, and shake . . . and yet remember. . . .

I walked into a room, the most familiar room of my life, and saw her from the doorway. How oddly she stood, in her blue nightgown, not stirring, not speaking, not seeing I was there. Why did she stand in that strange way? . . . One leg slightly back, a little above the ground, and one arm over her face, hiding the lower part, leaving the eyes to stare over it? And why so *many* Lauras? Three facing me and one, back to the door. The full-length mirror, three-paneled, held her form like some great, life-sized triptych, the Virgin, and she, Byzantium-blue.

Laura . . . I whispered the name, though my whole person called it out, she still silent, no sign she heard. I walked forward, afraid, as though this loveliness were yet some terrible thing. The upraised arm . . . so stiff . . . heavy . . . unresponsive in its arrested state. All three faces opposite watched while I searched the fourth beside me that permitted all this license and never moved. The grotesqueness . . . I wanted to flee . . . but three startled pairs of eyes were watchful while I stared at the arm, raised like a shield . . . hound-frightened . . . still.

It was no corpse, standing one foot up, one down . . . but what? I gazed on it fearfully, moving my hand as one would toward the deathbed, asking mute questions with finger speech. Those pained eyes, what had they seen in the mirror, or what had they asked? What did the arm hide, or what had it sought to stop? Graceful enough for a ghoulish ballet, the foot lifted in back . . . or an endurance-practice pose of pantomime—surely overlong now.

I touched the blue nightdress. Strange that she lived but felt none of the soft strokes of my hand on the soft fabric. I touched her flesh. Laura! . . . The name thrust out, screamed in her face . . . Laura! . . . Grasping the arm, pulling it, pummeling the up-

raised hand, the shoulders, the back, pounding the
wooden form to shake it somehow awake, stir it to
be. . . . The mirror looked back, my hectic, thrash-
ing arms, and hers, as though fending me off, three
times transfixed.

When had it fixed you? . . . Before bedtime,
while you stood to brush your hair before it on the
cold floor, and the light on you? . . . Toward morning, rising from bed, the mirror facing, drawing you
as all mirrors draw, pulling you into a camera? . . .
Voices . . . room silent . . . playwright asking,
"Which real? You? I?" . . . and no answer. . . .
Processions . . . children in dress-up, clap, do it
again, costume and cloak . . . young ladies, elocu-
tion, walk slowly, unhurried, turn, face audience, bow
low, gracefully, up, around, oh try it again . . . faces
. . . one rising, many ranged alongside, heaped one
on the other, and which one am I? . . . Three, separate, contending . . . "yes" to the right, "yes" to the
left, "yes" to the very center, "yes" everyone, yet hold
me, stop me, fix me in one, "no" to the shifting, the
moving, "no" to the flitting, the fleeing, the in and
out of me, stay hold close fix end and the stop of me

Part Three

(1)

THE place where Laura went was like a walled city facing the world from the heights. Its tall turrets were thrust out to meet the sun, and the dwarfed cottages were scattered on the flank where lawns ran down to meet wall, gravel-gray, high and thick like a fortress. Through the grillwork at the gate one stared with immense eyes at this relic of another time, desolate—seemingly abandoned, even by time, left to the merciless elements pounding alone at its doors.

A figure hurried along the road and a faint sound was wafted down the footpath. Only these signs pointed to the hidden activity within, but one felt life mysteriously present, secreted away to exhaust itself, carted surreptitiously from sight. The place resembled nothing so much as a barred medieval town where pestilence raged, and care was taken to preserve appearances, locking the plague tightly within until it had consumed even itself in its ruthless egalitarian passage. Everyone kept from the streets where affliction walked abroad in the daylight and anxious eyes peered down through slats and bars to survey emptiness below. One could see shutters fastened all around; only shadows fell on the glint of metal. Closer still, one saw figures leaning there and countless eyes searching the bright street from every side.

Still, one walked this beleaguered city, doing what one had to do, turning frequently toward the hidden faces up above that watched with such unexpected raptness the approach of any life, any new thing. One searched in vain for a single encounter to direct the footsteps, right off, to the destined place, and not disturb with unnecessary sound the unnatural stillness. Finally, one confronted with a mixture of relief and awe little white signposts that pointed the way toward clustered buildings, each one nameless, designated only by letter-number, cleansed even of the life façade of the word.

I was taken in by Laura's city, not as she was, but as a useful artisan, another hand to lift the daily crush of services extended with such helpless parsimony. Though I never mentioned her name nor barely thought of her outright, I walked its streets knowing she looked upon them from above, from among those faint shadows I saw suggested everywhere. I wished to know all there was to know about that madness, which, with little preparation, removed life from the hub of the world to such stark exile behind these doors.

That first day I was confounded going from place to place, shown one building after another, told regulation after regulation, led from this guide to that, to see how complete was the sway of this mad place, how much a community it was, nonetheless; its laws and government specially created to meet its bizarre demands. The guide left me, at last, before the old building to which I was assigned, one on which ivy had been started at one end but never grew.

From the outside, the unnatural calm persisted that, from the gate, had seemed to cover this whole hillside. But with the click of the lock all its caged, imprisoned sounds were unloosed. The heavy door swung closed, and a cacophony plummeted into the hallway from the rooms within, a peculiar, undifferentiated din like the vast percussion of the orchestra, granted license to sound unaccompanied, each member at once. I thought of nothing so much as of Dante accosted on the threshold of the Inferno by the terrible accumulation of all its sightless sounds. With as much foreboding, I entered the first circle.

To be locked into that world of the sick in mind with the door shut fast is an exacting imprisonment. Though you begin in full mastery over its conquest and its ravaged victims, in the end you are increasingly at its mercy, a petitioner at its gates, unless with an extraordinary bound you o'erleap the wall.

For that wall was very real, high so that you could not look out, thick so you could not look in. The most ordinary murmurings of life were sealed off by the stout stone wall and thick oversized doors, and only the uncommon, exaggerated ones remained to be magnified and reverberate through the heaviness of stone, concrete, and wood. Within, everything—not only sound—was exaggerated, almost a caricature of life. People, even those ordinary souls who partook of the outside life, going and coming from these doors, as one would to and from an office, were infected by its heightening, its oversized shadows. They were, on the one hand, either too good or, on the other, too evil, to be believed. Either they came, like Edson, to make of those obsequious sick shadows of men their body servants; or they remained, like Miss Beck, to minister to all their ills, nursing, coddling them like unfortunate children, wanting, as in the stories that she read, to work among lepers and prostrate herself on their sores.

These were the two extremes I worked with in my daily rounds, for they, too, ranged in and out of the crumbling, univied building where I was first sent. Ours were the hopelessly senile—old, too weak to strike at the plaster and drive wedges through the soft stone, as they might like. They sat in their chairs or stood by the windows, a legion of old men—arthritic, paralytic, delirious, peopling the universe with voices of men grown mad as they were. And we who cared for them walked in and out among them performing the menial tasks one must do for the very old, becoming, with habit, more accustomed to the distasteful ones, expected to sit at one's desk and look upon these battered men who babbled, slobbered, wet themselves; hid food, objects, feces; cried, hollered, whined, vomited to get attention; called you father, mother, God Almighty, as though these were the run of men, those their objects, and this the way of the world.

Were there no young people left, only these endless numbers of old men who had lost a grip on life, not yet ready to die, but unable to live any longer the small lives apportioned to them, nowhere to go? And where were their families? Surely there were mates, brothers, sisters; or had they outlived them all, as my grandfather outlived all who had had connection with the far, far years of his life that no one around him remembered, and so he might wonder if they had been, at all? Did these men leave families behind them almost as bad off as themselves, or had they drifted off from everyone, out of touch with relatives and friends for over a generation already? Sometimes I saw the checks that came in from their children and grandchildren, or the postcards they sent saying they could not pay, and I imagined them long since alienated from these distracted people, wondering why they must continue to help keep dead men alive, nourishing their stale bodies, abiding the abuse, the smells, the madness of the mad.

So, visiting days were quieter than the rest because there were enough who knew the waiting and the expectation to make it quiet, hushing, silencing the voices that lay in the ceiling, moldered in the floorboards, hung in the window-frames—oh, that chorus of disembodied voices that visited spiritless men, and that slowly faded, disappeared through the woodwork on visiting day when the living voices were expected to come and never came. The contrasting silence pounded in our ears, and at five o'clock, when no one else was permitted to pass the gate, they crept out—the voices unconquerable—parading and jeering, screaming at the old men who flung their frail arms at their nothingness and sobbed, falling more deeply asleep inside the blessed din of the everyday.

(2)

Y E S, it is all very well that I saw all those others
who had abandoned life, heard how they shut the
world out with their delirious cries—but what of me?
What of all of us, the others who cannot abandon it,
and must live the lives, nonetheless, that have become
so worthless in a world deformed by an evil chance
that raised one up to unbelieved peaks and dashed one
down again with as little care or notice? There was
rage in us, too, as much rage as there was in those
men and women who threw themselves upon matted
walls and floors, wailing their life wails, pitting themselves upon that smallest possible miniature world,
only to be tossed back by it, not bruised in every physical part of their being, but all the more dazed, left
with despair and rage intact, their greatest satisfaction
not permitted them—the taking of vengeance upon
the world and the destruction or mutilation of themselves—not even this wish granted them by a perverse
world that made them repeat the gesture a million
times without satisfying their desire. My rage was as
great as theirs. I could not see the frantic starting up
of one of them—suddenly aquiver, panting, throwing
himself without warning upon some quiet, unsuspecting neighbor, toppling him to the floor, flaying
him there, growling, moaning like some wounded
beast—without the sense that it might be a great joy
to run amuck, to divest oneself of that fierce hatred

of created things that were held so low, made so paltry by life itself. Surely I had as great a cause as they.

And yet what satisfaction could there be even in that? I saw them, these men and women who sprang up bursting within themselves to maim some living thing, perhaps as they, too, had been maimed in the secret, bitter hearts they hid in their vacant faces; and when they had flailed and pummeled a bellyful, they fell back again, hoarse and tired, and all that accumulated anger expended, they returned from their confinement quiescent, limp, still-living beings.

Knowing the uselessness of every feeling that I felt, I yet wished for their existence all the more. Might not some shattering explosion of my innards end the lassitude, puzzlement, helplessness with which I now lived my days? It seemed I was destined to *just that* thenceforth. With that desperate thought, my mind riveted on all those past times in which it seemed I had been moving ever closer to the full life that in early grandmother-swathed time was what the world was. With that passing, the sense of promise had left anchor, was set adrift, forgotten, growing dim, only to be rediscovered with the clearness and reality of a mature being on the ocean-drenched beaches of Pavilion Heights. Laura . . . the life I thought we might have . . . that passed so close to being! Was it ever true? Or were they really dreams, those moments of such exaltation, the eager wanting, cherishing of everything in life? Where were they now, if they existed, and where was that inevitable, warm flowing toward the full, happy life I envisioned the rest of my days to be?

Up from immersion in other thoughts came the

answer, rising up in a confused mass, a growing stridency on every side . . . the shrieking here; the sobbing, the moaning, the groans from there; the laughter, the squeals, the roarings, the peals, oh, the shouts and the curses, the weeping and wailing, muttering, sputtering . . . welling up everywhere, wherever I turned sounding louder, crescendo after crescendo, unending . . . the wonder of life! . . . hysteria around me! . . . what possible happiness, this grand design, fulfillment! . . . riotous screams at that. . . . All that chaos of sound, what was it? Nothing, nothing placed on the fulcrum side by side with my own railing and jeering, disillusion, despair.

It was truer than any world outside. What did I have in common with that world that never sputtered its pain? Out in its streets in the light of day, one might never know its corrosion. Though I knew in my mind that all these ragings and wailings I saw in my new everyday were ineffectual, satisfying no one, accomplishing nothing, yet they corresponded with greater reality to the hopelessness I resigned myself to. This cauldron seemed infinitely closer to life than those grotesque, unperceiving forms that maintained a sinister composure while the world crumbled and frothed at their feet.

Then it seemed to me, as the days and days slipped by, that, contrary to what I had first thought, it was not the surviving in that place that was so hard, but, once past the first encounter, ever leaving it at all.

(3)

SOME days in a place like that were very calm. If the sun was bright and the air warm, the lawns green, well kept, the footpaths clear, who was to take it for the house of the mad?

After lunch one might go for a stroll around the grounds. In the heart of the city, all this green, this countrified air, would be hard come by. And here it was, there for the asking, the gentle sloping of wide lawns down to the wall, and the brown, pebbly footpaths that interwound them.

Even the women in the small yards behind their buildings seemed less strange. One crossed the semicircular path for half its length and might think it a small park, part of a modern project, perhaps, with clusters of women scattered about, childless all of them, or at least one thought their children had all run off to play somewhere, leaving them here to await their coming. For they seemed on closer inspection to be doing just that, these women, waiting for someone or something only just left and expected to return imminently.

How content some looked, staring at one another, talking together as they stood close to the fencing separating them and me. How much some of them must have wanted company, for there they were, waving at any stranger, like myself, who loitered past.

Only when one looked more closely did one see they were not anxious urban women wondering where their children were at all, being far too childish themselves. There were some walking up and down, fondling some prized possession like a beloved doll or pet—a bit of string for this one, a shiny stone for another, and straight ahead, one with a moldering piece of crust she had become attached to. One perceived, as this one held hers up to view, that one sought to hide hers, that whatever that prized object, they had fastened on that one thing; everything turned on its endurance, on its meeting favor, as the child's world revolves on a handful of petty, perishable things.

There were some, too, who reserved a small space unto themselves, circling their domain fiercely, jealous and proud, moving back and forth, up and down, in sulky proprietorship—or no, more like glowering, caged lions bent on preserving a dwindling majesty.

Past them, one came upon a bench painted black, the one where often I liked to sit, lunch over, to enjoy, at least until it came time to go, the patch of outdoors spread on all sides. The sky was full of floating white clouds that one was told as a child don't really move, rather we do. If one closed one's eyes, the sun warmed the face, and a color flickered before closed eyelids, now red, now yellow.

I looked up from that small spectrum one day to find a lady in a trim straw sunhat smoothing her dress as she sat, unasked, beside me. She wore her own clothes, a sundress women might wear to visit, a bit more elegant than usual in that place. She was middle-aged, heavy in the body, and had a sweet face, heart-shaped, I thought.

"I used to wear this all the time when I was living." She glanced down at her dress as I had, speaking confidentially, sharing thoughts she might not tell everyone. "One of my favorite things for a warm day."

I smiled in return. There was something still young about her, an undiminished brightness of the eye, and she had rouged herself and fixed her hair more carefully than the rest.

"I should never have died," she whispered, pushing a loose hairpin into place. "It was so premature and unfair. You don't mind that I came?"

I shook my head, hoping she would speak again, for her manner was so natural, as though she had come out for tea and knew just how to make the best, pleasant conversation.

"I hate to insist so and push where I'm not wanted. But really, I should never have been taken so young. I told them time and time again, but they wouldn't listen." She sighed and turned farther toward me in her seat.

"Well, you see what it's got them. If they would only listen when they come—but no, they say, 'Now! Are you ready?' and never wait for an answer at all. They're quite dreadful!"

She began to giggle softly under her breath.

"They never thought I could do it. I said to them so many times, 'No, I won't come. I absolutely refuse to stop existing, just like that.' But when they come, they won't ever listen, no matter what you say. And of course, most people aren't so vocal when they're quite dead, you know."

Seeing that she frowned at something, I glanced up to where she looked.

"Oh, here's Miss Beck, the dear. But I did *so* want to talk with you. You look a bit like a young man I used to know. When I was living, I stroked his hair while he slept on the hammock in our summer house. I was very loving. You're not he, are you?"

She had risen and now took quick, short steps, almost a run, to join the other figure. She ran so lightly, one could barely believe she was more than a very young girl, lithe and slender instead of a little heavy all through the body, and so soft was her run, that for a moment she seemed as bodiless as she might have thought herself to be, judging from her conversation.

It was quiet when she left. The buildings seemed larger than before because they met the eye unexpectedly. On such days one wondered why they were there at all, some so imposing, others on the flanks less so. Might not everyone be turned out on the grounds to enjoy this raised countryside made beautiful in bright weather, instead of just the select few with everyday privileges and those others given free passage only on special occasions?

The women with nothing to do but wait stood in their little congregations as I passed. A few waved at me again. Drawing near the place on the footpath that was especially close, I saw that one of them took the same direction I took, on her side of the yard, a little in advance of me. She ignored my presence all the way, until suddenly she reeled 'round to confront my figure, yards away on the footpath, first menacingly, then smiling her satisfaction that she had caught, at last, the stealthy culprit in invisible pursuit wherever she went.

I liked these days when I spent part of the time out-of-doors. Then one finally lost the mass, had some sense of the individual. For then it was that they might be observed singly—one alone here, another picked out of a small group there, one even encountered on the path or met in the little store where they might go to buy some trinket or bit of food.

One woman walked along with me a little way, making every movement I did, showing a grave delight at this shadow that stood upright, that followed her out there where the grass grew.

Glancing at the time, I saw that I should go. Past the small dwellings I went. They were like large cottages where several families might live at once. If one looked in at the window, he might wonder why they were so especially secured and why some of those inside stood on such perpetual watch by them. There were one or two such faces, distinguishable because I passed close, before I saw the third.

Laura! Everything in me lifted up as always at sight of her. Her face, her figure leaning at the window, still unmoving, unaware, staring like that into the stir. If she could know me, smile, any sign she saw! No, I never expected it even. But it was Laura!—her face white, that soft whiteness bereft of pigment, I had finally found. And the dark hair, fluffy to the side, not quite gracing the shoulder, waved, and a widow's peak at the hairline. Not changed, none of the particulars altered one bit. She, suddenly there, performing what the strain of memory did imperfectly.

Laura!—months after, still unmoving, unattainable. Everything in me reaching out with my hand toward the window. Would she never in the world look upon where I stood, and all our happy times, our love, well up in her eyes? —Hazel, changing with the season, the day, the dress—changing always, as she would never change from that rigid staring. . . . I had to move or I might leap to the window, shake her again, do some wild thing.

I had begun to run. In all the quiet, there was a tap-tapping—not light, soft, a mere ripple of grass, like the lady, her straw sunhat not bobbing as she went. A loud pounding all the way down the path, pounding, pounding on the ground, in my neck, in my ears. My heart pushing ahead of the irregular thump of my feet, all else quiet, calm, unagitated out there. Her face flickered before my eyes with each lurch forward, almost smiling, but not even quite that.

I slowed down to keep it steady before me. Like a photograph it was! Click and it is done—life imprisoned, stopped in this fixed form, verisimilitude so great, almost an actual presence, duplication without life. What should one *feel* toward it, this thing that bore such great relation to the thing itself, but was only shadow some substance had cast? It bore a spell, some incantation, looking up with the expression of life from the dark regions of the photograph. But would one ever think to gaze on it in lieu of a living presence, as though the thing itself?

I had looked at Laura. Some image of her, surely, not her reality! But what other substance was abroad —the real Laura—this, then, a duplicate form? Had it been Laura herself, and I, reaching my hand to-

ward her, could not break the line of her gaze, disturb the stillness that enveloped her? . . . Laura!
A film of water blurred the image before my eyes,
dissolving it so it disappeared.

Now I was better composed, walked more lightly
into the stir she looked upon. Perhaps another day, I
thought, I will take the same path, and if all is as
today, and I wish it, I might come again to look at
her photograph.

(4)

EVEN there life did not remain the same. What
had been alien and strange grew increasingly familiar, the din and the chaos less than that first day with
the door closed, those accumulated sounds issuing
into the hallway. The locking of every door became
so much a commonplace that the turn of a knob giving free access into a room or building seemed, in
contrast, the peculiar act. Sometimes when I thought
of those first days, I wondered: was this the place,
or was it some other that had given rise to those
same impressions? This or that was odd, perhaps,
but what was there to be disbelieved, or to leave one
aghast?—and yet I remembered having had such
thoughts.

Even the people I had to do with every day were
less trying than I had formerly imagined. We became
even a family of sorts—an eccentric one, to be sure,
but still, we were more and more a distinct entity

unto ourselves, only set off and isolated from the world at large.

One could feel as great an absorption and as much comfort there as anywhere. One had to get used to other things, that was all. Granted it was not every day that one encountered grown men whose fantasies had stripped the outermost layers of their lives. Some, believing their animal selves to have acquired dominance over the man, accordingly fell to their knees, scrambling across floors on all four limbs in the frenetic enactment of their daily needs. If anything, they had carried a reasonable insight forward into a strained conviction and then a step beyond that into outright action. So one simply stepped from their path and let them proceed where they were going without interference, with no thought to take advantage of their reduced stature. Most of the others there had their own particular afflictions, and took neither thought nor notice of that of anyone else. But there was one among them, a young man not over thirty, who set himself as an obstacle around which a convinced quadruped would have to navigate. If he was not successful in deterring lugubrious or agitated movement through the room, he would plot new impediments, and if his upright form, arms akimbo, or a diverted chair did not accomplish it, he would himself assume, with a sly smile, some horned-animal form to butt the deluded ones from their course. He would sometimes subside into laughter when he had some cowering form trapped in a corner, and then step aside with assumed courtliness to allow him passage. This awareness of another's ills and knowledge of his own acts made me wonder if he was, in fact, only calculating these outbreaks to amuse himself and convince us of his madness. For at other times he could converse with such aplomb, even brilliance, that one wondered why he was there at all. I speculated that he did not care to leave that place where his prankstering, short of harming anyone, was left unremarked, and he, conceivably in full command of his faculties, was unwilling to surrender a life that afforded him a certain ease, even cushioned the irresponsibility dealt with so harshly by the outside world. Was it possible that such a one as he was as sane as I? Or was I perhaps beginning to be a less reliable gauge of reason than I once was?

There were others who convinced me at once of their true state; there was no denying them their madness. One man was possessed of such hilarity at all times that the effort of that vigorous laugh sent his body into short spasms which had not ceased since he arrived. Doctors milled about him from time to time, for his system could not sustain such unrelieved convulsion, and he was becoming progressively blue before our very eyes. And still he threw his head back, rocked back and forth on his feet, and the chill of his laugh burst out of him into the room.

There was, too, that illness that fed and fashioned the illness of others. If some in that place spoke not at all, and others just a little, there were always the few who made of the rest a captive audience, compensating for any lack of eloquence by their own abundance. So it was with the man who appeared in our midst one day, heavily bearded and with deep, red gashes in his palms. At great length he explained to everyone he met how, while in his pulpit, in a

sudden flash from above, in full view of his congre-
gation, yes, at the very words in his sermon, "The
Chosen of the Lord," these symbols of the faith had
incised themselves on his upraised hands. The clamor
that went up then, he would say, the cries of the
sinners beating their chests, sure at last of the punish-
ment he had promised them. But the evil in their
hearts—the evil of men, he interjected, was an im-
mensity undreamed of, boundless—that evil welled
up in their hearts again, overpowering the grace that
even at that moment was ready to settle upon them.
Yes, imagine the perverseness of mankind, disbeliev-
ing what they themselves saw with their own eyes,
a thousand times more torn by doubt and lack of
faith than that errant Thomas in the days of the
Lord. Then he held out his hands, the palms
stretched out before the dazed faces he had collected
together. And he bent over them, pressing them by
word and motion to their knees, permitting his small
flock, one by one, to kiss the scarlet wound.

Even knowing that we must watch him carefully
or he might implement his mark, I could not help
feeling, seeing him spread his upturned palms before
him, an intense suffering in his face and a Biblical
dolor engraved in his eyes, that that mark was part
of his whole bearing; naked of it, he would be incomplete. Yet it was mainly this that had separated
him from many another preacher with his flock.
Without that physical token of blessedness, without
whatever pressed him to make real that mark that
many others abstractly termed their calling, he might
be continuing these same sermons to a larger flock,
might have his own raised pulpit and not constrain

others to their knees in its absence. But, it appeared, it was exactly this excess that had exiled him from his parish and driven him here among us.

And those others who knelt in thrall at his feet? Who can say what his illness gave them, those leaning to bury their faces into his scarlet palm? They followed him sometimes when he stood alone in prayer, not sermonizing among them, and with devouring love gazed on those joined hands, silently begging their touch. What exhilaration rose to their faces when he disclosed them again, and held palms aloft for their homage! The Lord will mark you in His own way, he intoned, for He sees in the present-day Sodoms and Gomorrahs how few are the humble. He sees your faith and records it among the deeds of love. Then each rose, eyes glittering— whether at words or sound, who knows?—but with what rapture they passed to take up again some silent corner they had left!

You may well imagine my shock, then, at a new discovery concerning this very man. One day, as this same scene was enacted before me for the thousandth time, at the very moment when his little band effected a harmony of genuflection, he intoning over them, I saw his face closer than ever before. A look of such derision crossed it, of such knowing charlatanry, I looked the harder to confirm it. Yes, it was still there while those heads bowed before him, a passing through the eyes, across his smile, of his own disbelief kindled by those distraught others; his knowledge of what he was not, the forgery of palms, all these leaped into that brief look I intercepted while he blessed in such flagrant blasphemy the devout who knelt there.

Certain of what I saw, I felt, at sight of it, churned up in me buried doubts about this madness I found on every side, that in this man, of all the rest, I had so deeply believed. Was this madness only the sham one encountered every day in the wider world? Or did that intercepted look convey a moment of lucidity that flared up, perhaps, even in the most confused mind? For days I looked upon that man as one of the sane come to exploit the helpless credulity that flocked wherever he went. Yet I discovered a deeper madness impelled him to feign one form while he suffered another. Imagine my further surprise when I divined this splendid martyr had been in former times, to other inmates, once a renowned general, in still another phase an archcriminal, and in the one before the incarnation of a saint, each time knowing full well he was not what he claimed. But in the careful perpetration of each guise he laid bare in himself that further madness which urges itself upon more gullible natures but in whose machinations was implicit the deeper malady.

Still another day I circled the silent grounds until I came again to Laura's window. She stood at the very place where I had left her, unmoved from her vigil between my first coming and this. Lingering there, I felt no wish to leave her, nor any thought, as on the last occasion, of abandoning a longer stay. My desire for her was enacted in a straining forward, as though an effort great enough might tear those eyes from stares upon a vacant space. I leaned so far in her direction that someone seeing would have thought me one long inclined plane. The reaching out was not only of my hand but of my whole being that joined the gesture in its longing to catapult beside her. I tried to push on to a meeting ground that could suffice to stir her to some act of knowing. With only the smallest push forward, a movement that extra bit farther, I might force the gates of her world, plunge myself over that narrow crossing that was the real restraint, keeping her there within, me here without, apart so long as I resisted the impulse to be of her world.

If only I did not stand aloof as now, watchful, gazing, but rather could place my questions that had grown so loud, so imponderable within its very door, could carry them over the threshold to join the enormous chorus that swelled from within, and then could be left there.

I swayed, feeling myself less and less separate, feeling drawn into that Babel of tongues that addressed the universe and were themselves unburdened of reply . . . that edge of reason, so abrupt a line, so deep a gorge. I, too, wished to make a crossing. Gazing upon that immobility that was Laura, I knew I wished it. My desire to join her was articulate, clear for the first time . . . if only even momentarily it would give some answer. Or, disregarding that, if, by whatever means, it could anchor again a life set adrift by her going, and those questions that came, wave upon wave. Or, if not to anchor . . . for I asked no impossible . . . if, even only this much . . . for however short a time—not to know oneself anchorless.

(5)

W A L K I N G once through that wider room full of agitation, that undirected unrest that bubbled over and erupted now and then, I came upon an alcove set off from the rest, a place of calm where gentle air enveloped three figures within. Lamps had been set inside, intended for work at close range, and this different, directed glow spread over the archway, filling that alcove with a warm illumination, foreign beyond its reaches. A quiet emanated from it, tranquility not expected in such a chamber as that, and I further saw that two of the figures were seated within, one to each side of the central one. Curiosity led me to approach, for I had not come that way before. Pressing through the milling bedlam to the arched opening, I drew close to that anteroom, and noted in passing how scrupulously the others kept from about that doorway. One man stopped and gripped my arm as I neared that arbitrary line separating it from the rest, and shook his head. Another whispered mysteriously, "Not there! The mad one is inside!" I passed with greater curiosity to see who it might be the mad thought madder than they.

To my amazement it was a face I knew! Never expecting to confront another familiar being in all that place, here I was looking at someone I had last seen perhaps three, even four years before. Then as now he was seen from a short distance, a disheveled

form not in harmony with life that passed it on all
sides, again heedless of stares and whispers directed
at it. That massive head—I remembered from that
day when any act of homage, however small, impressed—was now flung back against a chair, the
gray in the hair not uniform. That, his locks falling
in all directions, so unevenly gray, more than anything placed over his person so distressing and cha-
otic a look. His head was disproportionately large,
one in which the forehead protruded, and his eye-
brows, bushy, and they, too, streaked, hung on the
very rim. Seldom would one pass such a face without comment; strong and sharp, surely only some
mischance would keep it ungraven in marble, gran-
ite, or a tough-grained wood.

On first glance, it seemed he napped there, head
back against his chair, hands gripping the ends of
the chair arm, and the two who sat with him were
silent, leaning forward in their chairs the moment
he reopened his eyes. They listened with strenuous
absorption to the words he attenuated one after the
other between reflection, and glanced at the pages
that passed back and forth from one to the other.

How was it possible he was there, sitting as though
he belonged in that very place, taking occasional
note of some gyration or other in all calmness, before lapsing again into that bland disinterest? The
two who flanked him, on the other hand, cast around
them uncomfortable glances at everything that
erupted from without their separate alcove, or if no
specific thing diverted their gaze, they sat rigid in
their seats, afraid to look beyond the arch at all. He,
however, showed no sign of his discomfort or strange-

ness, and remained impassive in his seat while the others took up their papers and in my presence took their respectful leave.

It was true, then, that he was of that place! I reared up where I stood at the thought. Was it possible the greatest mind of our troubled time could sit there in isolated splendor in the place of the mad?

He raised his head, hearing my startled sound so close.

"What do you see, me or my papers?" On the table to the side lay several volumes and some loose sheets, and it was as I saw them that his imperious voice rose.

"My work continues here, imperfectly. But it goes on, as it must." From a more resigned tone, he became more jocular. "There are more papers, even here." He lifted a basketful of crumpled sheets, and held one up to me in mock auction.

"Here is one. Barely thirty words on it, a bit wrinkled and smudged. But that will add color, bring the higher price in the marketplace. This one especially so—*finite* crossed out twice." With a mock gesture he gave it into my hand.

"I bequeath it to you." Then in a more serious tone, placing the basket in its place, "That is what I leave in lieu of a life, sheet upon sheet, a life's work. But who will know the life?"

He looked up into my face, searching it the first time, his eyes screwed up in shrewd, confident appraisal.

"Are you familiar with the physical sciences? I thought not! That's very bad. It could be passed over in *my* time, thought specialized, but in these!

What will you ever do?" He seemed genuinely concerned, overwrought even, at thought of my bleak future.

"Surely you know the leading names—at least that much, especially the nuclear field. Whole lives poised on the circumference of their minds. How exciting to receive what they give! But they themselves, those pioneers? The common denominator I've found! Those human sacrifices! Yes, yes, exactly that. The very element they have so joyously harnessed, tamed, given back as a new power at the service of the world, that very element, even at the moment of highest exaltation and new discovery, invisibly passed over into them, burning in unnoticed passage into their entrails, along their bloodstream. Imagine the shock of finding oneself, so far from victorious over a chastened Nature, its victim! What man could conceive such grand irony, such judicious correspondence?"

His voice rose to a more excited pitch.

"May I not turn this observation also upon myself? Think what it was I explored—tamed, even. That mind of man I spent my life examining—to take just that! *That* is the master stroke. Yes, I concede it is. For it is, after all, the final corrosion, and conceptually a wholly worthy thing!"

Here he rose from the seat and advanced two steps toward me, his voice suddenly acquiring an hysterical shrillness as he moved.

"And you? Do you know who I am? Do you dare to look in the face of the great philosopher? I—the one whom the world has thrown off. Yes, that very world I faced in a new direction. *I* fashioned its future course. It takes, and then casts out at its first chance the one who gave the tools." His anger broke into a hard, bitter laugh.

"But I laugh in its face. I know who I am and what *it* is. And I am a willing exile."

As he stood there, his rage and jubilation vying to distort his face, I backed off from him to the archway, and as he broke again into his bitter laugh, I turned and ran through the room, his screams and laughter echoing behind me.

(6)

O N L Y a little more, I thought, noting the greater ease each day brought in those surroundings. Not too much farther to reach and I am there with Laura, where I will be happier than now. Not to strain again. . . . And my mind would drift into anticipation of that coming time.

Still, until then, I would note what passed there. I grew to know better those I saw, caught sight of them enough so they were like the people in one's neighborhood that one assumes to be there, takes for granted in any thought of one's domain without having to recall each separate one.

The woman in the straw sunhat passed. I waved even before she saw who it was. This time it was like seeing some old friend out of the past who now strolled nonchalantly on one's present street.

"Oh, young man, it's you." She smiled in her soft

way, touching my arm lightly as she passed.

When the Queen came to our building, I got to her before she made the rounds to me, so eager was I to see her. Her dusky Negro face was powdered a chalky white, and she wore always the same small, ruffled cap that in another place, another time, women wore to bed. Yet, sitting on the very back of the head, a border of lace standing around it, it seemed very queenly. How were her subjects, she would ask, and beg us to tell her outright and not shield her from the truth of things because she was a Queen. They were troubled times, she said, and it behooved a Queen to know, even if it meant being more familiar than she might have liked. Here she wrinkled her nose in aristocratic distaste. She would do what she could, she would say as she was about to leave, giving a final sigh.

One could barely pass The Old Man—everyone called him that—without his trying to stay your walk with his cane. So old, so lame was he, and yet he tapped along with that shriveled stick, proud that he could get about, speaking too loudly into one's ear, as though the world were deaf, while he, even at a hundred and three, had, in contrast, preserved his hearing. Quite a specimen, he would say. If all men could be like him it would be a different race—at over a hundred and three hardier than men half his age. They were mollysops, didn't know how to take air into the lungs and space it out. One could hear him tap, tap along the main walk and know when it slowed that he had stopped someone else with the end of his cane and had the same words for the newcomer.

These encounters broke into the day. It was pleas-
anter somehow to have a visit with one of them.
Did it matter if visits here were shorter than most?
Still, one had that fine sensation of having met others
in the course of one's day, and it had always perked
me up, even outside, when I casually met some
known person not expected in my travels.

(7)

THE excitement began the very moment we said
there would be a lawn party that day. A buzzing
started at the words, an agitated whispering among
those to go. We had not told them too soon before,
for we saw even in our late announcement how much
anticipation and anxiety moved them. Too greatly
stirred, some would surely have worked themselves
into illness if given more than a day's wait.

Not all could be invited, for it was held outdoors,
of course, and only those strong enough might go,
any whom one felt could stand the strain, enjoy it
fully, neither be undone by it nor spoil it for others.
So care was taken in the asking to keep it reasonably
small but grand, this celebration. If all went well,
there might be others planned someday, larger than
this one, but the weather could seldom be so fair.

By late morning we began to make things ready.
The first inroads into the silence of those lawns
spurred us to greater effort, and we grew more bent
and eager for their transformation into a festive place.

In swarms of three or four, we set up long tables for refreshments and spread and smoothed, with unaccustomed patience, the white cloths. We hung streamers from the trees, twisting them carefully and fastening them securely. We set lines across to join the nearest trees and made to dangle there bright trinkets the sun would catch and the wind spin to the astonished pleasure of the guests. The silver Chinese bells that tinkled as they spun would please them most. As one last preparatory touch, we found white lawn chairs with patterns of filigree work, and these we scattered in groups away from the tables so that they gave the right casual, informal look.

But though our preparations and bustle out-of-doors had seemed extensive, it could not be placed beside the hubbub that had spread inside. Some of those invited had asked for the first time for clothes worn when they came, and thought of themselves in their going-away dress made them more animated than ever before, and they pressed those forgotten remnants of the past to their faces, against their cheeks, and thrust them again at arm's length to examine them anew with their eyes and memory. Still others, as soon as they knew of the party, begged for new things to wear, and if it could be arranged and relatives would come, with what expectation and delight they waited and finally opened the bag or box brought them with their unknown finery! Squeals of pleasure came from their beds, and they waved their arms, gesturing for others to join them and see.

Some of the men had worn their faded blue shirts so long that the first feel of polished white against their backs and along their chests brought mysteri-

ous smiles to their faces. With what fascination they
stroked a finer garment against the skin when it had
touched their bodies, and their awed faces shone
with some rediscovery this simple act had kindled.

Then the combings that went on! Both men and
women brought out their combs long before dress-up
time, and with their incessant partings and smooth-
ings, endings and new beginnings, they appeared by
party time, for the most part, overplastered and over-
brushed, like small boys and girls done to an extra
turn for their first big social event.

But the ladies who had already spread out their
lipsticks, powders, and rouges were less animated,
for theirs was an air of concentration and intentness.
Some had been given mirrors the first time for this
occasion, and they remained poised in curiosity and
renewed interest at that reflection, seen after so long
an absence. So thoroughly did they examine themselves, they seemed to be looking into their very
pores; a few in attitudes of utter frustration had held
the mirror too close and could not see their reflection
properly, nor execute their make-up with satisfaction.

Of them all, the powdering was easiest, for it was
hastily done only a few times over. Even the rouging
was got over with fast, for they found in the mirror
the spots where it should go and then did not notice
they had overreached them when they dabbed their
own pale cheeks. But it was the application of the
lipstick, the remaking of the mouth that was the
tour de force. They took such painstaking care, such
lengthy consideration in this subtle art, and not in
the most fashionable salons could their single-minded

efforts be surpassed. Innumerable times they thought all was prepared, but it was not yet time, and they returned again for one last stroke. But the waiting was past at last, and they sat with folded hands, as though the party were already over, even as they were told that it would now begin.

They looked so proper, the ones who went, small pockets of dignity and fashion amid that larger unconcern and poverty in dress. And those who stayed looked on bewildered at this excess of activity, stood admiringly back as the others filed out, or passed them with a dazed stare at such peculiar goings-on. Some who realized asked if they might not go, too, and nodded, so easily reassured, when told perhaps the next time it might be they who were asked. A few wept that they remained behind, and begged to watch outside. With promise of some small trinket, their sniffles subsided and they withdrew, happy to think on their coming surprise.

All ready, the procession of guests moved inward from their buildings, out to the wide lawn, newly trimmed, especially green from its last watering, which had left by now no moisture but an added crispness. Dots of color proceeded to converge from all sides to the elegant tables, now overflowing with cookies, tea sandwiches, and cool drinks.

All the magic of those transformed surroundings rushed to their amazed faces, lit now with the realization before them of what might have remained another excessive dream. Some walked on tiptoe, fearful of dispelling enchantment with too heavy a tread. Others could not tear themselves away from that first sight of laden tables, brilliant streamers, and the trinkets they could with a stretch of the hand send spinning and tinkling overhead. But there were a few, more poised, who took refreshment at their ease amid the glitter, and who moved with much assurance, almost at once, to the outlying lawn chairs, white and dainty, that had been placed in small, circular array.

"I'm glad you could come," said the Queen to those who passed. Then to a neighbor she confided, "I worried it would rain, but look how fine it's turned. Do sit down," she urged, and waved them to their places, as though they had not already sat there, sipping their lemonade as she came up. With a grand air she placed her arms on the sides of her chair, her back straight and not quite back against the seat.

"It's my public duty," she addressed her assemblage there. "My subjects wait for it each year. If only they understood about gardens!" She pointed in the direction of the tables at her more deplorable guests.

"The Lord's abundance, and we unworthy to touch it!" The martyr with red gashes in his palms passed to one side, holding his hands out to the sky, intoning in a mystic trance and watching from the corner of his eye to see the effect.

"Drink and eat at your peril, unless you have cleansed your soul!" One or two guests who heard seemed puzzled at this chiding tone, and set aside in bitter disappointment what they were eating.

"Please sit down, young man," put in the Queen, waving him to an empty seat. "You're blocking my view."

The lady in the straw sunhat smiled at him as he

moved to her right. The martyr looked stunned at the bright blue of her sundress, and with a touch of modesty she put her hand to her breast where it was low at the bodice.

"When I was alive I lived in a house with wide lawns, almost like this. How they must miss me!" With the first show of sympathy from the martyr's eyes, she hastened to add, "We weren't rich, but learned to live pleasantly. My poor Charles worked so hard that we might have that house, and I was always careful to keep it up. I planted a rose bush to the side, and just before I died, I made an English border out in front. I only put the babies'-breath beside the columbines the day before they came. —How nasty that they spoiled it!"

"We must renounce the world!" the man to her right intoned, leaning toward her bosom from which a sweet fragrance rose.

"What a dreadful thing to say!" And she looked genuinely hurt, tears filling her eyes. "I was so loving, and now they're all alone. Why should they take me? I was young and loved life, even the pain of it that filled my head sometimes. How could I give it up? I would not cease to exist, even if they took me so unwilling away!"

The man beside her turned up his scarlet wounds to view.

"Cast out the love of man." He made his words impassioned, and she started up at sight of his marked hands.

"Heavens! How terrible that you're hurt." Taking her handkerchief in some distress, she laid it across his exposed palm, and tying it to the underside of his hand, she smiled with a new flood of warmth.

"Play all you want, dearest, but do be careful. When you get hurt, I hurt, too. You are so much to me, my son. I waited that day you came with such excitement. So do take care. There are so many hurts I would save you from. If you could hear me—oh, my dear—though I am dead!"

The martyr gave her a curious look, as though she had kindled something deeper in him, and all his impassioned warnings set aside, he raised his arms to either side, one hand still loosely bound, dropping his head to one side like the Great Martyr he suddenly knew he could be, and suffered almost unmoving and with a faint smile the woman who dropped to the grass beside him and pressed her head in his lap.

"No, no!" said the Queen rising and pulling her up. "Not on the grass," as though this were the essence of bad taste.

"And young man—" she turned to him imperiously—"I think you ought to go. Nothing but troubles since you came. To the tables and out that way!" She pointed the direction in some heat.

"I am the King of Kings!" cried the man, moving deliberately to his feet.

"Oh, how intolerable! Take him out at once!" The Queen motioned to onlookers who stared at the scarlet palms held high to keep them away.

"Come, my dear," put in the lady in the straw sunhat. "A cool drink and you'll feel better." And off they went, she leading the way, shielding him with the arm she had placed over his shoulder.

"There the prophet, here the king," chuckled the

philosopher who had come on the scene and stood now a little behind the Queen's chair.

"I hate to get cross." The Queen had not heard him and returned to her seat.

The Old Man tapped his cane slowly, rhythmically, up and down in place beside her.

"Footsteps. The men marching. Closer. Closer. Near now." His tapping grew louder, and his voice alternately boomed and grew soft with it.

"Another minute and they'll be here. The quiet. A long war done with. People pushing in the street. There's the hurrah—'Here comes the President'— and he walked by. A slim giant. The sun in his eye and his face screwed up." Here he motioned the Queen with his hand.

"Phoebe, get the flowers ready. We must throw them high or they won't reach. Just look, he's caught one in his hand. Think he'll smile when he looks so cross? He's waving the flower back. He so tall and we so small. Less than five you were, Phoebe." The Queen smiled and nodded.

"Nothing so grand as that—President Lincoln come, smiling at Phoebe and me. A hundred years, a century. Phoebe and I hugging close, never so glad. That we grew old, and nothing ever so grand again." He saw the Queen once more and leaned toward her, rocking back and forth with his chant.

"Hard times and dying, all that dying, and we so old. Who's to know the President smiled in our faces and waved our flower?—Phoebe, Phoebe, don't leave, don't leave just me." He reached toward her. "We two—running the fields, finding the flowers, twining the reeds." Here he took the Queen's hand in his, bending far over his cane, and singing imperfectly in a quavering voice some old song of his childhood. The Queen laid her other hand over his, humming the strange song, a syllable or two behind, and they seemed, those two, in their unintelligible duet, hand in hand, for just that moment to be warming the same memories while they sang. Once it was over, the Queen clapped hands.

"That was fine, fine." And The Old Man slumped back in his chair.

"Next year I shall plan entertainment. Everyone will sing, and we will dance all over the lawn. —Do you think it might get too wild?"

The philosopher moved off to the side and spoke to himself, out into the air.

"I am mad . . . they are mad . . . we are mad. How can I know it and still be mad? *They* don't, but *I* do. Aware of everything—up until the very moment. I shouted only yesterday. What did I say? And today, watching and seeing, so calm."

The lady in the straw sunhat had come back alone.

"Do find a place to sit," offered the Queen. *"There's* one that's free."

"I won't die like they did." The Old Man moved up in his seat, his voice loud again, vigorous, as though none could hear.

"There's no keeping them off." The lady in the straw sunhat sighed and sat beside him.

"I'll give them a taste of it." The Old Man thrust his cane in the air, slicing it feebly.

"They'll never get me. I'm a hundred and three." His voice suddenly shrill, almost a quaver.

"Hasn't it got warm? I'm soaked all the way

through." His new neighbor fanned herself with her hand, rose, spread out her dress again before resuming her place.

"Move along, move along." The Old Man pushed a shadow off with his cane.

"Don't be cross with the children. They never *mean* to do wrong." The lady in the straw sunhat was hurt again and cried softly into her hands.

Up from among the tables, over and across the lawn came a small procession. The young man, recently martyred, trod heavily on, both hands held to either side, palm out, to form the famous sign that now eclipsed his former show of supplication. Four or five followers already trailed behind as he came. The lady in the straw sunhat raised her head at their steps, and seeing him, waved and brightened.

"What, has he come back?" cried the Queen. "This is treason. He will pay for it."

Now he had reached the middle ground among the circle of lawn chairs, his arms still the arms of the cross, his red wounds showing, and his head hung to one side.

"How fraudulent," commented the philosopher, throwing his head back to laugh. The man opposite him raised his own head at the sound, met the other's amused gaze and, arms still outstretched, joined with a low chuckle. The laugh, at first soft, became more open and loud, even growing hysterical as it rushed out. The devout who circled him did what he did, laughed because he laughed, and the infectious sound spread to the whole gathering, fanning out from the circle of lawn chairs, passing from one to the other, reaching farther and farther, to encompass the last table until everyone was laughing.

The entourage moved on, but the lightened mood they had brought prevailed. The Queen forgot her anger and asked for more lemonade. The philosopher passing it around received smiles and attention for the first time.

"You've never been to my parties." The Queen was grateful that his manners were so fine. "You may sit beside me," she smiled.

But The Old Man would not give up his place. The philosopher shrugged, not caring, and took up a station behind the Queen's chair before she could get cross again.

"I don't suppose you know who I am," he whispered over her head, but she had not heard. "Why are there none to know it?" His voice was raised now, and he addressed everyone or no one in particular. "Who knows who it is that stands here?"

The Queen was craning her head to see him. "What is the trouble back there? Come out where we can see and hear you."

He passed from behind, in between the lawn chairs, and took the middle ground for himself.

"I am a philosopher. Do you know what that means?" He pointed his finger from one to the other, and people moved forward to see what the excitement was.

"One in a century. *I* am that *one*. The great mind of the modern age. —What delusions of grandeur, even my own, compares to my greatness? —You, and you there, do you know who I am? Who has changed your world? Who revolutionized its thought? —I!" He was fully shouting now and gesticulating wildly with his arms. "It was I! I! I am that man!"

Those nearest were tittering, but others farther back laughed outright, and soon the whole lawn rang again with their laughter, this time everyone straining in one direction, toward that one ridiculous figure, head flung back, in their midst.

"I think everyone's having a fine time," observed the Queen, much satisfied at the success of the outing, seeing everyone so gay.

"Is it really you, Louise?" The Old Man pitched his voice very low and leaned toward the lady in the straw sunhat whose breasts peeped out when she stooped for her purse, dropped in that burst of excitement.

"Lovely as ever," he whispered. "So white, shaped for the hand to hold. Didn't I hold and hold you at night?"

"Oh," she drew in her breath and sat back. "The love of the night."

"We kissed. That first time, bright day. But the barn was cool where you waited. —You, the first, the only love of my life."

"Oh, how we kissed! You holding me hard against you, so I thought we might snuff out our lives pressing so hard. Your strong arms."

"So strong by day, but soft in the nighttime. Your touch made them weak. The passion . . . up through our legs . . . down from our lips. Love of the loins, Louise."

"If we put all our love in it, we will make a child. A child comes from love, leaving one body, stretching to join the other, life caught in between. We will make a male child tonight."

"No more, no more, Louise. My legs don't ache any more, my loins so light. All that passion spent. We are too old, Louise. No more. We look strange, comic. Even remembering. They will laugh that we loved once—we grown so old, no love in us. But how we yearn, remembering. Never to have you, Louise."

"Yes, how could I forget that love of the night? And I so loving. Charles, alone in that big, empty bed. The touch of the sheet so cold when you sleep alone. —And still they took me! Who will sleep in my bed and make it grow warm?"

"That place is the first to die." The Old Man pressed the cane between his legs. "So cold it gets."

"I will tuck in the children and then come." The lady in the straw sunhat still whispered as she rose to tiptoe away.

"Don't leave me, Louise. —A hundred and three, and no one to talk to."

"You're raising your voice again," admonished the Queen from the other side.

"But nobody hears," he said, pitching it higher.

"Nonsense! —We can't give them headaches. They wait for it all year, and I won't have you spoil it." The Queen glanced toward the tables. "They're beginning to push," she frowned.

They were growing so lighthearted, so lightheaded from the joy of it, roaming over the lawn, seeing the trinkets dangle, and the tables filling as soon as they thought it was over. They could not help the little cries that occasionally rushed from them and the giggles that followed. One burst of laughter around them was too much to bear, and all that had been

held in as tightly as possible tumbled out at the first
chance to join any riotous sound.

Now some were jostling, making their joy touch
someone in moving the elbow, rubbing the shoulder.
Some had begun to dance, only a rocking, a pulsation
forth and backward in their places. But some had
joined hands with others, and now in a string, five
had started to run, hand in hand, follow-the-leader,
circling the tables and pushing onto the lawn. A
clapping broke out; chanting rumbled from knots of
people who were pressing together and who—moved
by the tension, the upsurge of wild spirits spreading
among them—dispersed one by one to make their
own way, one waving his arms here, another shuf-
fling in dance there. Now a few had run from one
tree to the next, sending the Chinese bells tinkling
into the air, spinning them faster, faster, until only
flashes of silver whirled by, only a glitter circling so
fast, and the tinkle growing into a jangle of sound,
a high-pitched clanging poised overhead. Short cries,
sustained screams rushed to join it; the line of running figures, hand in hand, grew longer, ran faster,
zigzagged from one side to another wildly. Some
pressed forward to join their spirited dance, some fled
their coming, and others set themselves awhirl in
their own joyous dancing, spinning around, twirling,
abandoning themselves to the wide lawn, not caring
about the small collisions, the clots of people they
broke apart, sent sprawling with their windings and
whirlings, their spinnings and twirlings. Without
direction, without care, unmindful they pushed, they
tumbled, they hurt, no one responsible, no grand design, running, dancing, silver bells clanging, push-

ing, lurching, randomly spinning, pitching and reel-
ing, a haphazard jumble of movement, of sound.
Streaks, colors, whizzing by, revolving. . . .

Laura—one more push to join you. Who said
death was this, a spinning past, one's whole life revolving? Surely it was rather madness, the buzz and
the whirl, a directionless flow, randomly pitched.
And I, too, if ever to be suspended as they were suspended, if ever to be stranded in advancing and receding tides of swirl, would have to plunge now, be
catapulted this very moment, sucked up forever in
the enveloping swirl.

Why was it, rather, quiet and still—not a person
seen, not a voice, not a whisper? The wide lawns
emptied those minutes thoughts poised on the swirl.
In just that time empty of queens, philosophers, martyrs, old ladies and men, all led off, gathered up, contained again by the inside, directed world. The long
tables, bare now of food . . . white cloths soiled,
awry . . . the streamers dangling in air, flapping
white, red, yellow against trees, trailing ground . . .
a bare rustling through bells, the only whisper, of
wind chastened by lull . . . and I among them.

I—aware as I always had been. The oneness with-
stood even the swirl, a tongue of fire dancing the waters, undrowned. There was no sucking me in. Why
did I exult so? There was to be no Laura. No ex-
ultation in that, but a new sense, a clearness: She is
off out there, a photograph that will always be still,
down on the other side where cottages stand on the
footpath. I will not see their little brown roofs, I
will not see the long shape of the window, I will not
see her again.

She ran there out of my eyes, down my cheeks. Why was my whole life gathered in tears that ran, melted on air? They had been so few. One cried so seldom, and then found floods stored in him. They burst out once, twice, three times a lifetime, all the cries, the lostnesses buried in rivers, rampaging, free. They came now for my whole life: Tears unshed by my grandmother's bier; I knew she was dead. Unshed by the mirror; would I never say: she is gone, nothing to save her?

I said it now. She was beyond recall. No striving could unlock the door. If all life is this sadness, these tears, a crying out at empty tables, torn streamers, silent bells, why do I feel it so strong rushing to my head? Why do I feel one with the throb of the veins measuring me out to the universe, my hum?

I held everything in the cup of my eye—the green of the lawns, the blue of the sky, the white, red, and yellow of streamers, gray turrets, brown roofs. They, too, part of me, as those others, those loved things, are part of me, and yet thrown off, too, ejected in each crystal reflection that ran off, melted in air.

I closed the gate softly, for I was the only stir in the silence. Yet I wished to stir softly, gently, not violate with my leaving this short, blessed calm that had saved.

(8)

THIS is the very present. Rain falling that has fallen for hours, heard now when the monotonous *tap-tap* destroys itself in a sudden hurling against window, and I look up.

I sit in my room, aware my thoughts have been trailing off, the most recent past tapering until, imperceptibly, we are living the new moment, and some rushing against window, some stir in the room, wakes us to it.

Yet the rain was here when I woke, but exiled to that part of morning which says: it is Saturday, it is drizzling, it is a day at home. It blended so inscrutably with the past that the newness seemed continuous with it, remained unnotable, until a lunging like this forced the head up: this is the very present.

The wind gathers, blowing and stamping on rain; the sky sinks from its gray to a blackness; a thunder roll drops from its midst. Somewhere people are running, seeing skies darken, rain quicken, hearing a dreadful thunder. They scatter, searching skyward for a yellow flash that, even expected, comes oversoon, lighting heavy pockets of cloud. Streets, returning to nature, become rivulets; walls are washed clean. Trees tremble for plumage wind has whipped loose. Between sky and earth no margin; all has become one moist descent.

I saw it close, that blurring of forms, horizon

slipped so far, it has soaked in the earth. A boy, I lay by a lake, throwing in pebbles, twigs, watching them cut water, drown in rings their splashing had made. Wind blew against water, rippling wide circles, as if an invisible hand, far larger, stronger than mine, were discharging lightly its fistful of stones. The clouds sank as low as they might, horizon dropping, fading before eyes. One might sleep in it.

But I heard sound: water fallen on water, welcoming its own, the first growl of thunder, and ran with the rain falling, woodward, to reach the clearing beyond, some roof. So many trees. Overhead a bridge of leaves, pelted, borne down upon by this shower of stones, swayed, holding off sky, imprisoning rain. Underfoot those that had fallen clung to the step. The woods darkened; the birch trees became their heavy, black bands. Boughs, whipped loose by the rain, crashed; my own fear that came to my lips dissolved into that single tremor of forest sighs, earth rumbles—my cry indistinguishable from theirs.

Tripping on swollen root, slipping on perished leaves, where was my sound? In the progressive silence I heard it—the *tick-ticking* of feet, like the beating of an insignificant clock in the immeasurable time of the universe. I stilled it to meet the sudden hush that was spreading. Hardly a bird called or cried or sang. There was barely a movement of leaves. The wind abated. Wood voices stilled . . . trees tenantless . . . shrubs unrustled. Only the echoless, the silent, the void.

Then it burst from the heavens—the thunder clap potens—rumbling and rolling, a giant roar and a mighty quake, a lusty reverberation tumbling a yellow sky into forest darkness. There was a flutter among trees; a quiver ran through them in a common swaying. Only the ash tree was still; nothing of it moved or bowed to break its dark silence. I saw an angry finger of light part its leaves, crackling in deep fury as it sundered that majestic head and plunged itself forcefully into its bowels. I saw it die. In an instant the tallest, loftiest tree in the forest—no more, instantaneously disrobed, shorn of its leaves, clipped of its boughs, stripped of its bark. It remained blanched and naked, gripped by a deadly pallor, a corpse already, and I could see the black disfiguring scar where it was disemboweled, gleaming in its chalky flesh. Yet it remained rooted in earth, as though it were yet forest, still of its world, though less tree. Another monstrous crash of thunder shook the sky, and with it the storm lost force, dissipating as quickly as it had struck.

How many trees in the forest are reclaimed by the Nature that made them? Standing without, who sees them, those blunted tops, broken boughs, hollow trunks that fill the forest? There they stand, covered with the sores of a painful blight, still rooted to the fertile earth that conceived them, no less forest for their passing. Their hulks endure until the forest can cremate its corpses, sometimes hundreds of years after death, when they have, at last, worn away all evidence; disintegrated, they are ground back into the earth where they had lain as seedlings, returning to the conception bed to father new life in their turn.

The moist earth that slides through the fingers, how many lives has it been, how many forms has it taken, while histories mix their silt with the river?

Bits of root and flat of stone, they underlay the forest: ocean beds grow on them. They have become the soft clay of generation, womb of the universe.

Each single life a small instance, each moment an eternity that cries out against the measuring palm. Who is it counts time? The wind flings sand, grinds boulders, incises mountain faces, takes those captive grains and buries them into the earth, or carries them to the soft underside of clouds where they drop unseen in raindrops to the place where the wind sought them. The river bends trees, strips twigs, dissolves roots, lays them at the foot of the forest, where they had dreamed to be in final union with the earth.

The claim of death, how short a thing, almost as short as life. We fear its violence, yet it has what we seek. The crimson berry glitters in the sun, wishing to stay always crimson, always plump, always berry; yet what is there to fear from the bright-eyed bird sent to pluck it from the bough, warming it in the soft belly? The common rosemarie knows: she grows more beautiful, luminously white, exposing a bare head to the approaching foot that crushes its life juice.

I am that berry, that sturdy rosemarie, that buffeted grain, that tender root, that lofty ash. We live, yet fear not. It is all the same to us. We have loved what we have been. There is no terror in becoming. Let other men struggle, let them deny, resist. I live, hearing the stilling tread, seeing the quieting finger, not cringing at its dark step. I will be ready. My neighbor, screaming, is welcomed; my father, unfulfilled, is beckoned; my son, unborn, is taken. I wait.

Afterword

A Bridge of Leaves was first published in 1961. It is a beautifully conceived and written work, a classic novel of development. Diana Cavallo began to formulate her ideas for this novel after she had written a series of six or seven short stories. Finding the short story a rather confining genre, Cavallo broke out of the form in order to expand her ideas on the education of a young man who seeks to make the fragile crossing from the self to others. Cavallo's lyrical prose reveals her love of poetry and her minimalist but powerful scenes reflect her passion for the theatre.

Indeed, *A Bridge of Leaves* can be read as a drama in three acts in which the narrator, David, explores his relationships in the family, in the college arena, and in the mental asylum. Each setting (or act) prepares David to cope with the deep and abiding grief that he experienced as a child. Early in the narrative, David describes the world of human memory as "one, vast rebirth." Throughout the novel, Cavallo explores the power of memory to heal and restore. David's capacity to withstand his losses reinforces the strength of memory to console without torturing. David realizes that without memory lies madness; he comes to this understanding when he unsuccessfully tries to annihilate his sense of self in the mental ward. David survives his loss of twin, grandmother, and lover; he does this by allowing the language of poetry to transform the pain of his loss. His attendant sufferings as a survivor prepare him to embrace the world without fear: "There is no terror in becoming . . . I live, hearing the stilling tread, seeing the quieting finger, not cringing at its dark step." Cavallo extends a bridge for her sensitive and loving narrator, so that he may enter adulthood stronger for his suffering, like the mighty ash tree in the forest, which remains rooted still in earth, even after death; like the "sturdy rosemarie," which grows more beautiful after its life juice is crushed.

Diana Cavallo was born in Philadelphia. After graduating from the University of Pennsylvania, she worked briefly as a psychiatric social worker. As a witness and observer, Cavallo wrote the case histories for patients in preparation for diagnostic sessions. Not only did Cavallo interview the patients at a mental hospital, but she spoke with family members, too. What Cavallo continues to recall about her work in the asylum were the keys, the locked doors, and the faces in the windows of the patients' rooms. Each image is carefully incorporated into *A Bridge of Leaves*, exquisitely transformed by the requirements of the imaginative process. David's decision to work at the mental ward is intimately related to his inability to accept his loss of Laura, his beloved, the actress who cannot separate herself from the Pirandellian and Shakespearean roles that she plays on stage. Laura succumbs to madness, transfixed by her image in a three-paneled mirror.

That David's ultimate epiphany occurs within the confines of the asylum forcefully suggests the murky relationship between sanity and insanity, the blurred boundary between those on the outside and those on the inside. For a character like David, the trip into the first circle of hell is necessary to understand the process of creation. David discovers a "oneness" that is able to withstand fragmentation, confusion, and sorrow. Despite his overwhelming desire to join Laura in her madness, David is finally able to unlock the door of his own grief in order to discover it anew and transcend it. Able to "close the gate softly" on that necessary part of his life, David leaves the world of madness without ever forgetting it. From each experience, David re-creates in his memory the vital and sustaining aspects of his life, which will help him grow into a fully mature adult living in the world.

To achieve a satisfying adulthood, David must first learn to mourn his grandmother's death, the person with whom as a youngster he most closely identifies: "my grandmother's was the first inner world I discovered. I felt her pulse before I knew my own; lying against her chest I could hear the rhythm of her life in the crease of her neck, and I took it for my own which was silent in the child's world of becoming." Still a young boy when she dies, David is confronted with his parents' failure to utter the decisive word "death," to explain what happened to his grandmother. Although David comes to realize that his grandmother is "truly and forever dead," he postpones grieving for her until he reaches the full flowering of his adulthood, which occurs for David when he is nearly thirty years old. Throughout his early adult-

hood, however, David regularly recalls his grandmother's facial gestures, her hand movements, her
"Mediterranean homesickness." In fact, after making
love with Laura at an abandoned lookout near the ocean,
David recalls in Laura's gesture of pushing back her hair,
the long-ago face of his grandmother, "plucking strands
from her forehead . . . hands moving in rapid strokes,
kneading, crocheting." Laura's presence connects David
not only to his childhood memories, but to the memories
his grandmother shared with him as she was "lost in
thoughts of another sea, blue and faraway." Immigration
to a new world unmoored David's grandmother, who
ceaselessly felt like an exile in America. Empathizing
with his grandmother's loss (of country, of language, of
customs), David seeks to find an anchor in Laura, who
joins "old love" with new.

Old love comprises the family narrative of Part
One of the novel. At age six, David discovers that he is a
twin, his brother Michael having died at two years of age
before David could consciously remember him. When
David is accidentally mistaken for his twin brother, his
awakening into the dualities of his nature begins: "Out
of this submersion for an instant came consciousness of
that other dead self, the lost blood stream, the complementary nervous system, the dissolved will, my brother."
Throughout the narrative, Cavallo repeatedly employs
words and phrases such as "entwining," "twining,"
"doubled over," "so doubly so," and "twice-lost," to name
a few, in order to interrogate the notion of a single,
unitary identity. David's identity is reinforced by his
status as a twin who believes that in moments of estrangement, "there rises in me the stamen silk of Michael, born

to the world, reclaimed, made unborn by it, but still borne in me in that one vast rebirth, the world of human memory." During his passage into adulthood, David re-enacts the dualisms informing his identity in his relationships with friends outside the family. These characters reflect David's loss and his confusion about how to develop an identity that is both separate from and interdependent with his early losses.

Part Two of *A Bridge of Leaves* focusses on David's college education. Time away from the pressing environment of the family allows David to join in relationships centering around friendship and love. It is truly during this section — the lengthiest of the novel — that David engages the powers of his human memory. His thoughtful ruminations about his aged Philosophy professor, his sterile dorm room, and his burgeoning connection with a college friend, Phil, reiterate the family narrative of Part One. As David struggles to "extend a bridge" between his past and present, and between his solitary self and his longing for companionship, his memories provide him with the materials for creation.

David's close friendship with Phil and his love relationship with Laura reflect his seminal relationships with Michael and his Italian grandmother. Moreover, during this section, David struggles to understand the profound significance of his early, tragic losses — of his twin and his grandmother, neither of whom he has fully mourned. In Part One of the novel, Cavallo has David describe himself as "overlaid with what I have become." During Part Two of his formal education, David becomes the archeologist of his own cultural and familial past, digging beneath the surfaces of his daily life. What he finds there, down deep, is potentially annihilating: his own desire to be subsumed by his bottomless guilt and grief over the premature death of his twin and his paralyzed inability to mourn his grandmother's death.

Cavallo examines this longing throughout *A Bridge of Leaves*, but one scene in particular anticipates David's capacity to be healed, not destroyed, by his grief. During a walk home on a clear, dark night with his new friend, Laura, David points out the stars, Castor and Pollux, also called Gemini, the twins. Urging him to speak further about their story, Laura simultaneously encourages David to reaffirm the inexorable connection between the sons of Leda and his own twinship: "Well, their devotion was the main thing. Inseparable to an unbelievable degree. Far from the ordinary bond. They were each other's complement . . . if that explains it . . . To make the story short, death spared one and took the other. For the survivor life was unbearable, 'he living, Castor dead.' " The single quotations around David's final words denote that he is quoting another source, but the unidentified pronoun "he" may also refer to David himself.

Furthermore, by "reading" the meaning of the stars, David constructs himself as a text, embedding the story of his loss into a known story. This interpretive activity allows David to place himself squarely within a literary and historical tradition of love and loss. Although unable yet to identify himself fully within these traditions, he has employed a vocabulary of loss in which to contain his grief. For David, constructing a story about his loss both orders his confusions and heals his wound. It may very well prevent him from becoming ill.

However, not until Part Three of Cavallo's novel, the narrative of madness, do readers observe David fully accepting his duality of selves — as a twin and as an Italian American. David's acceptance prevents him from succumbing to madness, which is the fate of Laura, his beloved. By their very nature, narratives about the descent into madness profoundly disturb. That Cavallo incorporates such a narrative within *A Bridge of Leaves* reveals her awareness of the dangers of development. David falsely (and dangerously) assumes that Laura is his complement, his "other part at last," his lost and grieving self. When Laura becomes catatonic, David is brutally shocked into revising his belief that his beloved is solely his complement. In fact, David enters the "walled city" of the asylum as an employee in order to clarify his identity and to end his search for a complete self through another person. What David learns within the confines of the institution is ultimately useful to him: it allows him to determine his role as an individual with a future in a world outside the static environment of the asylum.

When David first enters "Laura's city," he is filled with the excitement that guides an initiate, hoping if not to save Laura, then at least to join her in stark exile from the world. To convey the riskiness of such a journey, Cavallo describes David as a modern-day Dante, accosted on the threshold "of the Inferno . . . With as much foreboding, I entered the first circle." Echoing his cultural ancestor, the narrator invests Dante's odyssey with modern meaning: madness is a kind of psychological hell, in which the inhabitants are wholly circumscribed by their ceaseless suffering. Like Laura, they are stopped in time and unable to shape any form of a future around the past.

Cavallo ingeniously incorporates an episode of celebration toward the conclusion of David's stay in the institution. Cavallo herself calls this section the Mad Lawn Party Scene; the conversations that ensue among party members on the lawn of the asylum interestingly parallel Lewis Carroll's chapter — "A Mad Tea Party" — in *Alice in Wonderland*, a connection that Cavallo made herself during our discussions about her novel.* Like the Mad Hatter, who bemoans the fact that it is always teatime, David enters the lawn party aware of the fact that the party-goers are frozen in time, speaking out of turn, and utterly devoid of the ability to make conversation with anyone, despite the Queen and the Old Man's "unintelligible duet."

Although David tries to join their saturnalia, he comes to realize that there remains within him, however fragmented, divided, and alienated he feels, some "oneness" that withstands "even the swirl, a tongue of fire dancing on the waters undrowned. There was no sucking me in." Appropriately, Cavallo employs in one image a dual reference to the holy spirit and a maelstrom. The image re-connects David to his Catholic origins and perhaps even to his successful negotiation through his mother's birth canal. He will not succumb to a madness that marks the death of his consciousness. David's temporary withdrawal from the outside world — so central to the theme and structure of the *Bildungsroman* — enables him to incorporate the knowledge of his loss into a future decidedly part of the social world. David's close encounter with madness revealed to him the same psychic process that accounted for his necessary withdrawal and return.

To describe David's return to the outside world as an achievement of "oneness" is potentially misleading. David's recognition and acceptance of his losses signals his consciousness, but as Robert Scholes has explained in *Protocols of Reading* (1989), "above all to be conscious that one is conscious — is to be split, differentiated, alienated." David can look at himself in the mirror and see his "reflection properly," recognize the duality in his nature and understand his development. He can close the gate softly on this experience in his life, without forgetting or being terrorized by it.

In a letter written several years ago, Diana Cavallo explained that the title of her novel spoke to an issue of abiding concern — that of identity: "its very name, *A Bridge of Leaves*, while taken from the text itself in the ash tree episode of the finale, is meant to suggest the extension of the self into the other, the communication and communion with the world outside ourselves . . . a bridge, yes, but fragile, perishable, but still all we have in taking the risk of reaching out beyond the self."** Cavallo employs the image of leaves as a reminder of their nature: they may fall and die, but they also nourish the earth out of which new life will grow. Such is David's quest: to learn of his fragility, but fearlessly to reach out for new life. The republication of Cavallo's 1961 novel is yet another reaching out. It is a novel superbly written and constructed; it is as much about individual development as about broader issues such as ethnic and familial identity. Its references to Pirandello and Dante reinforce Cavallo's own love of the theatre and her Italian cultural heritage. Her novel-in-progress, *Juniper Street Sketches*, is devoted to building a bridge between the self and others, America and Italy, the healthy and the sick. It a composite work depicting Italian-American neighborhoods and Italian locales such as Tuscany, Florence, and the Abruzzi. *A Bridge of Leaves* is a testimonial to her exacting abilities as a writer of immense imaginative skill.

Mary Jo Bona

---

*Phone interview with the author, November 18, 1995
**Personal correspondence with the author, July 23, 1991.

AGMV
MARQUIS
Québec, Canada
1997